Corey traced **cheek and,** **night air, Ly** **expectancy at his mere touch.**

She was struggling to breathe now, terribly so, her body burning with awareness. It was only a kiss, but it held so much promise, such a teasing, tempting glimpse of the man she was starting to adore, that it took all her strength to finally pull her lips away.

'You have to go,' she whispered, reluctance in every word.

'I know,' Corey said, equally reluctantly. 'But you know I'd give anything to stay?' His arms were still wrapped around her, the swell of her stomach pressing into him, and Lydia nodded—because she did know; she knew exactly how he felt.

This was only the start…

PRACTISING AND PREGNANT

**Dedicated doctors, determinedly single—
and unexpectedly pregnant!**

These dedicated doctors have one goal in life—to heal
patients and save lives. They've little time for love, but
somehow it finds them. When they're faced with single
parenthood too how do they juggle the demands and
dilemmas of their professional and private lives?

PRACTISING AND PREGNANT
Emotionally entangled stories of doctors in love
from Mills & Boon® Medical Romance™

Recent titles by the same author:

THE CONSULTANT'S ACCIDENTAL BRIDE
THE DOCTOR'S OUTBACK BABY
THE BUSH DOCTOR'S CHALLENGE

**Look out for Carol's next book—
next month in Modern Romance™!**

THE PREGNANT REGISTRAR

BY
CAROL MARINELLI

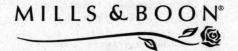

MILLS & BOON®

All the characters in this book have no existence outside the imagination of the author, and have no relation whatsoever to anyone bearing the same name or names. They are not even distantly inspired by any individual known or unknown to the author, and all the incidents are pure invention.

*First published in Great Britain 2004
Harlequin Mills & Boon Limited,
Eton House, 18-24 Paradise Road, Richmond, Surrey TW9 1SR*

© Carol Marinelli 2004

ISBN 0 263 83920 6

*Set in Times Roman 10½ on 12 pt.
03-0904-46074*

*Printed and bound in Spain
by Litografía Rosés, S.A., Barcelona*

CHAPTER ONE

TAKING a steadying breath, Lydia would have loved to press her face against the cool bathroom tiles, to rinse out her mouth and splash her face with some icy cool water, but the shrill bleeps from her pager merited no such luxury.

She was sure morning sickness should now be horrible distant memory, sure that by five months she should be able to walk into a hospital without diving for the nearest rest room.

Why did the books always get it wrong?

Catching sight of herself as she darted out of the cubicle, Lydia gave a grimace. She'd assumed by the time she hit registrar status that she'd sweep into the ward in chic, well-cut suits and impossibly beautiful shoes attached to thin silk stockinged legs. Not dashing in like some overgrown heifer with baggy theatre blues covering swollen ankles. But the tailored suits she'd envisaged for this stage of her career didn't equate with the subtropical temperatures of the special care unit and high heels didn't make for a speedy dash along the corridor. The chocolate curls she'd so neatly tied back this morning were escaping rather alarmingly and she'd have loved to have fiddled with a bit of lipstick, would have loved to have put some blusher on her way too pale cheeks, but there really wasn't time. As a very new junior registrar on Special

Care, the shrieks from her pager could only mean one thing…she was needed, and quickly.

Consoling herself that the last thing a tiny baby would care about was whether the doctor had lipstick on, Lydia wrenched open the bathroom door and practically flew along the highly polished tiles, popping a mint into her mouth as she did so and praying her unfortunate delay would go unnoticed or, more pointedly, wouldn't have done any damage to the fragile lives that were now in her charge.

Racing through the black swing doors, even though she'd just washed her hands, even though time was of the essence, protocol still had to be adhered to and Lydia squeezed a hefty dose of alcohol rub into her palms as she scanned the special care nursery, watching the crowd huddled around a crib as she deftly made her way over.

She'd so wanted to look cool for this, had wanted to breeze in on her first day supremely in control, to dispel in an instant the questionable merits of filling a three-month maternity leave position with a rather pregnant doctor. But instead of arriving cool and unflappable, it was a rather pale, shaky Lydia that made her way over to the gathered crowd. 'What's the problem?'

'No problem,' a deep voice clipped, and Lydia looked to the moving mouth on a very tall, very wide-set, very annoyed-looking ogre dressed in theatre blues. His green eyes worked the tiny infant, large hands retaping a probe connected to the baby's rapidly moving stomach, each tiny fast breath requiring a supreme effort. 'The drama's over.'

'What happened?' Lydia had to wait a full minute

before she got a reply. The crowd was drifting away now and a nurse fiddled with monitors as the avenging ogre suctioned the baby's airway with surprising gentleness for someone with such large hands.

'Prolonged apnoeic episode.' Those green eyes finally met hers, and he flashed a very on-off smile. 'Extremely prolonged, hence the emergency page.'

'I'm sorry about that,' Lydia mumbled, realising the direness of the situation she had just missed. Apnoeic incidents in Special Care were part and parcel of the day. These tiny babies often seemed to forget to breathe which would send most staff into a spin, but here under the controlled setting of Special Care it was routinely dealt with. Lydia was used to having a conversation interrupted as a nurse gently flicked the bottom of a baby's foot in an effort to stimulate the infant into breathing, then resume the conversation as if nothing had happened. An emergency page wouldn't have been put out lightly and Lydia knew that from where the man was standing there really was no excuse. 'I got here as quickly as I could.'

'You're the new registrar?'

Lydia nodded. 'Dr Verhagh.' She knew she should have given her first name, knew her rather brusque response sounded a touch standoffish, but she was desperate to exert some semblance of control here. 'And you are?'

'Corey Hughes. I'm the nurse unit manager.' He shook her hand briefly before turning back to his small charge.

'Well, Sister Hughes,' Lydia ventured, watching him stiffen slightly, as male nurses often did when their formal title was used. Hell, why hadn't someone come up with an alternative title for a male nurse? Lydia mused while attempting a recovery. 'I mean, Mr Hughes,' Lydia corrected. 'Is there anything I can do here? Though it looks as if he's stable now.'

Checking the infant's observations on the monitors, Corey gave a rather curt nod of his head. 'It's all under control. It was a mucous plug causing the apnoeic episode. We've suctioned his airway and he's doing well now.

'And by the way,' he added with a crisp smile that didn't meet his eyes, 'the name's Corey.'

'I'm aware of that.' Lydia flashed an equally brittle smile. 'But I prefer to save first names for the office and staff room. Out on the ward I think it's more reassuring and less confusing for the parents if we call each other by our professional titles.' She could feel the colour whooshing up her pale cheeks. She hadn't meant to come across as quite so brittle, hadn't wanted to so forcibly erect the barriers on her first day, but something about those green eyes was unnerving her. 'So if you'd rather I didn't call you Sister out on the floor, is it OK if I call you Mr Hughes?'

'Well, if we're going to be formal…' Corey flashed her a dark look '…then it's actually Dr Hughes.'

'Doctor?' Lydia frowned, her brown eyes darting down to his name badge. 'But I though you said you were the nurse—'

'Unit manager,' Corey finished for her. 'That's right. I also have a doctorate in nursing, and from the confusion it's obviously caused you, I'm sure you can appreciate how difficult it would be for stressed parents to have to listen to me rattle off my résumé every time I introduce myself, so if it's OK I'd prefer you to call me by my first name.' As he stalked off, Lydia let out a low, weary breath. It wasn't actually the best start to her first day, but just as she thought her rather brief dressing-down was over, the avenging angel paused and turned. 'Could we have a brief word in my office, before the rounds start, please, *Doctor*?'

His office was appallingly untidy, mountains of paperwork cluttered each and every available space and Lydia was forced to stand for an uncomfortable moment as he flicked on the kettle before moving a mountain of notes from a chair then gesturing for her to sit.

'Can I get you a drink?' Corey offered.

'No, thanks,' Lydia declined, not too keen on a repeat dash to the toilet, but her refusal obviously lost her another brownie point as Corey shrugged and made one for himself, spooning in three massive teaspoons of sugar. Leaving the teabag in, he made his way to the desk.

'Have you been shown around?' Corey started, and Lydia nodded.

'At my interview, though I wouldn't mind a quick refresher.'

Corey nodded. 'I'll take you round the patients as soon as we're finished here. The formal doctors' round isn't until nine, so it might make things a bit easier for you if you've at least briefly met them before Dr Browne does his rounds. He doesn't make too many allowances and the fact it's your first day won't stand for much when he starts firing questions.'

'Thanks.' Lydia gave a small appreciative smile. Dr Browne's temper was legendary—the fact Lydia had been working on the other side of Melbourne didn't mean she was completely out of the loop. The great Dr Browne's reputation preceded him, but even though she was rather nervous of being the target of one of his scathing comments, her nerves were over-ridden at the prospect of working alongside such a fabulous mentor.

'About this morning,' Lydia ventured, determined to set the tone, to push aside the rather awkward initial greeting and forge a more relaxed working relationship. 'If I came across as rather formal—'

'I don't have a problem with formal, Doctor.' Corey broke in. 'What you like to be called is your business. I happen to prefer to work on a first-name basis, but that's my own personal choice. I can understand where you're coming from and if you choose to keep a distance then that's fine by me, we all cope with things in different ways, but for my part I've found being on first-name terms fosters a better relationship. The parents are generally here for a long time, particularly with premature infants, and despite the initial slight confusion as to who's who it's how I prefer to work.'

Lydia gave a small nod, even opened her mouth to speak, but he clearly hadn't finished yet, continuing before she even got a word out. 'However,' he barked, 'I do have a problem with doctors who don't respond promptly to an emergency page. I've got two new interns who started last week and they weren't exactly a lot of help this morning. When a baby goes off, you know as well as I do that experienced hands are needed, and quickly. The fact a registrar was fast-paged meant that a rapid response was called for.'

'I know,' Lydia agreed, 'and I really am sorry.' She hesitated. The last thing she wanted to do was play for the sympathy vote here, to tell this rather arrogant man that she'd had her head down the toilet as her pager had gone off. No doubt he'd roll his eyes, no doubt he'd mentally voice the question that undoubtedly begged—was a pregnant doctor really up to such a demanding job? But even though she'd rather be considered unfit than uncaring, Lydia still didn't speak up and it was left to Corey to conclude this difficult conversation.

'Well, thankfully there was no harm done this time. The emergency was dealt with and the baby's fine, but next time you receive a fast-page...'

'I'll be here,' Lydia said firmly, meeting his assured eyes with a determined glare of her own, grateful for a tiny reprieve when the door flung open and a young nurse breezed in.

'Sorry to interrupt. I need your signature, Corey.' Waving a drug chart under his nose, the young nurse looked over and gave Lydia the benefit of a very nice smile.

'I'm Jo.'

'Lydia,' Lydia responded, aware of Corey's eyes on hers and trying to beat back a beastly blush as she dropped her title.

'Welcome to the madhouse.' Retrieving the chart from Corey, she made to go. 'Are you feeling better?'

'Sorry?' Lydia looked up sharply as Jo gave an apologetic shrug.

'I saw you dashing into the toilet, I doubt you noticed me. I, er, think you were in rather a hurry. If you need a cuppa or anything, just call. Corey makes it like treacle, not exactly the best thing for morning sickness.'

There was the longest silence after she'd gone, filled only by the sound of Corey filling another mug with tea and thankfully pulling the teabag out before it assumed mud-like proportions.

'Sugar?'

Lydia nodded. 'Just one, though.'

'Why didn't you say?' Corey asked finally as he placed a steaming mug in front of her, watching as Lydia took a hesitant sip, closing her eyes as the hot sweet liquid hit its mark, warm and soothing and, thankfully, staying put. 'Why didn't you just say that you weren't very well?'

Lydia took a deep breath. 'I didn't want you to think I was making excuses.' She gave a brief shrug. 'Look, the hospital's been fantastic. I can't believe I got the job, given the circumstances.' She registered his frown. 'Pregnancy doesn't normally work in one's favour when looking for a job.'

'But it did in this case?'

Lydia shrugged. 'I've got a full-time position for three months while Jackie Gibb's off on maternity leave, and then, when I come back, we'll job share. Dr Browne was forward thinking enough to realise that, rather than lose Jackie altogether, job share might be the solution. Most part-time jobs are filled by mothers.'

'Which you soon will be?'

Her rather nervous smile didn't go unnoticed. 'Apparently so.' She looked down at her softly swollen stomach, disguised under baggy theatre blues but still pretty evident none the less. 'I've got four months to go.'

It was Corey frowning now. 'I thought morning sickness only lasted for three months or so.'

'So did I,' Lydia groaned. 'Apparently I'm the exception to the rule, though it's not as bad as it was. At least now it's living up to its name and only confined to the mornings.'

'You had it pretty bad, then?' Corey asked as Lydia grimaced.

'It was awful. For the most part it's gone now, but for some reason, within half an hour of stepping into a hospital, no matter how well I feel...' She gave a rueful smile. 'I'll spare you the details. But once it's over, it's over, at least until the next day.'

'Must be the smell,' Corey mused. 'My sister used to say just the smell of the place made her feel dizzy every time she came to see me at work.'

'Used to?' Lydia looked up, hopeful Corey was about to reveal his sister's secret, a remedy perhaps that she hadn't heard about, but from his stance she soon realised she'd picked up on something rather personal and dropped the subject as Corey deftly ignored her question, standing up and gesturing towards the door. 'How about I give you that handover?'

Taking a last quick sip of her tea, Lydia stood up and for the first time since their awkward meeting they managed a simultaneous smile. 'About before,' Lydia started, but Corey waved a large hand dismissively.

'Forget it. Now, I know there was a reason...'

'I—I meant the first-name business,' Lydia stammered. 'I really do prefer Lydia—I don't know what I must have been thinking.'

'Hormones.' Corey winked.

'That's a terribly politically incorrect thing to say.' Lydia grinned, stepping through the door he held open for her.

'Oh, there's plenty more where that came from.'

The same light-hearted chatter continued out on the ward, from Corey at least, various nurses looking up and smiling, introducing themselves as Lydia slowly worked her way around the room. Lydia tried to smile, tried to come up with the odd witty response or friendly greeting, but it was as if her mouth didn't know how to move any more. She could feel the sweat on her palms as she dug her nails into them, feeling horribly awkward and exposed and praying for a fast forward when all in the unit was familiar.

Special Care Units were intimidating at the best of times, but Corey obviously ran the place well. Somehow there was a balance between quiet efficiency and relaxed friendliness which was no mean feat given the direness of some of the babies' health and the anxious parents taking each painful step along with their child.

'Patrick Spence.' Corey stopped at the incubator where they had first met. 'He's six days old now…' his eyes moved to the little boy still struggling with each ragged breath '…which makes it your one-week birthday tomorrow, little guy.' Rubbing his hands with the mandatory alcohol, Corey put his hands inside the incubator and stroked the tiny infant's cheek, and such was the tenderness in his touch Lydia felt her breath catch in her throat. They had stopped at every incubator, Corey had regaled the most painful tales but not for a second had he erred from professional detachment.

Till now.

Handling of sick infants was kept to a minimum, yet here was Corey gently stroking this baby's brow and there was an expression on his harsh, sun-battered face Lydia couldn't read.

'We normally save the cuddles for Mum and Dad, but this little guy's missing out on both counts,' Corey offered by way of explanation, his eyes never leaving the babe. 'But we're more than happy to fill in, aren't we, Patrick?' Clearing his throat, he pulled his hand out, fiddling with the oxygen-flow meter for a moment or two before carrying on.

'Patrick's mother arrived at the labour ward in advanced second-stage labour. She'd received no antenatal care and a rapid labour followed. Born at thirty-two weeks gestation, as well as being premature, he was also small for dates. Multiple anomalies were noted at birth and on investigation he was found to have major cardiac defects.'

He was silent for a moment as Lydia read the cardiac surgeon's reports, along with endless reams of ultrasounds, chewing thoughtfully on her lips as she did so. 'He'll need surgery,' she murmured, 'and preferably sooner rather than later.'

'Or later rather than sooner.' The irony in Corey's voice wasn't aimed at her and Lydia didn't have to look up to realise that. Babies this sick and this small were a constant juggling act: drop one ball and the whole lot came tumbling down. To survive, Patrick needed his heart defects corrected, but for his tiny body to make it through the complex surgery he desperately needed to gain some weight and stabilise medically if he was to stand a chance. 'Twenty-four hours after admission his mother became agitated, and was finally diagnosed as suffering with alcohol withdrawal. Valium was given and the drug and alcohol liaison service notified.'

'Patrick has foetal alcohol syndrome?' As Corey nodded, Lydia looked back at the small babe. Foetal alcohol syndrome was one of the few completely preventable causes of congenital anomalies. The babies suffered various levels of handicap, from mild learning difficulties and facial deformities to cardiac problems and marked retardation, but from Lydia's brief assessment of Patrick, his visible anomalies didn't entirely fit the picture. Heading to the wash basin, she scrubbed her hands before examining the babe more thoroughly.

'Have we sent off for a DNA work-up?' Lydia asked, examining Patrick's hand and feet, peering closely at his face and taking in the almond-shaped eyes and low-set ears.

'We have,' Corey responded, and for a second as she looked up Lydia thought she saw a flicker of admiration in those guarded green eyes. 'What do you think?'

Lydia gave a brief shrug but it was far from dismissive. 'He looks like a trisomy baby; of course Down's syndrome is a far more palatable diagnosis title than foetal alcohol syndrome, but in this case I think it could be both.'

'It's a tough call,' Corey said thoughtfully, 'but I'm actually glad to hear someone say it. As soon as

Jenny, the mother, started to show signs of alcohol withdrawal Patrick was basically labelled as an FAS baby, but I think it might be a touch more complicated, I guess we'll have to wait for the labs, and on current form we could be waiting another couple of weeks.'

'How is his mother coping with the news?'

'She won't come and see him. Apparently Jenny's admitted she has a problem with alcohol and has agreed to rehab, but to date she's refused to come and visit Patrick. She's talking about putting him up for adoption.'

Which was far easier said than done. The world seemed to be crying out for healthy pink babies but a handicapped child with special needs would take months, years even to place.

If ever.

'What about the father?'

Again Corey hesitated. Handing her a wad of notes, he gave a small shrug.

'What father?'

His two words said it all.

Glancing down at the patient notes, she read quietly for a moment. Patrick really had had a difficult start to life. Not only was he born eight weeks before nature intended, with major health problems, he had succumbed to several of the obstacles premature babies faced. His immature lungs had meant he had required forty-eight hours on a ventilator but he had been weaned off that now and was breathing with the help of continuous positive air pressure, a direct, measured flow of oxygen, commonly known as CPAP, but his marked jaundice was still proving to be a major problem and Lydia rummaged through the unfamiliar order of this hospital's files, trying to verse herself on Patrick's relevant issues.

'Here.' Taking the notes, Corey turned to the back of the folder, locating the blood results for her in a second, not even acknowledging the quiet murmur of thanks Lydia imparted as she studied the blood-work closely. Despite the intensive phototherapy to correct his jaundice, Patrick's serum bilirubin was still rising and her forehead puckered in concentration as she plotted his results on the graph before her. If they couldn't get the levels down, Patrick would need an exchange transfusion to remove the toxic blood and replace it, which would hopefully prevent organ damage.

Corey was obviously thinking along the same lines. 'It's an uphill battle at the moment, but we'll get another blood result around midday and hopefully there will be some improvement.' His eyes moved back to the little baby and they stared for a solemn moment at their small charge, watching the almost transparent abdomen rising painfully up and down with each rapid, exhausting breath, his face grimacing with the pain and effort of merely staying alive.

'Do you ever just want to take them home?'

'Heavens, no!' Her response was immediate, a sort of knee-jerk reaction, an instant erection of the barriers Lydia created just to survive her work. But even as the words left her lips Lydia realised how awful she must have sounded, watching the tiny headway they had made disappear in a puff of smoke. As Corey's eyes narrowed, she realised he hadn't actually expected an answer, that he had been talking more to himself than to her. 'I mean...' Swallowing hard, Lydia gave a helpless shrug. How could she tell him she was having enough trouble getting her head around the fact she'd be bringing her own child home from hospital in a few short months, let alone someone else's? 'I just try not to get too involved.'

When he didn't respond she pushed on regardless, trying to somehow rewind, to wipe the slate clean without revealing too much of herself. 'It's sad and everything, awful actually...' Her voice trailed off, realising how awful she was sounding, as if she had a plum in her mouth, hating the sound of her own voice as she reeled off a few more platitudes while knowing it was useless.

Unfeeling bitch.

She could almost feel him punching out the letters as he labelled and pigeonholed her, but as Dr Browne and his entourage swept into the ward the rather uncomfortable conversation was left behind as Corey gave a small eye roll. 'Ready for the off?'

The ward round took for ever. Dr Browne was rather old school and even Lydia was slightly taken aback by the in-depth discussions at the cots, sure the barrage of scenarios he detailed wouldn't be very comforting for the anxious parents. After a rather gruelling hour it was a rather washed-out Lydia who finally sat down at the nurses' station, simultaneously clicking away at the computer and wrestling with a mountain of notes to write up the ward round findings and formally prescribe new courses of treatment as the junior doctors set to work on the barrage of tests and drug charts that needed completing. Looking up, Lydia noted Corey quietly making his way around the unit, talking in turn to each of the parents, presumably answering the multitude of questions the ward round would have thrown up and hopefully clarifying a few issues.

He was good, she had to admit it. Most NUMs would be dashing off to a meeting or holing themselves up in the office by now, but Corey had barely left the shop floor all morning.

He was good-looking, too.

Where that thought had appeared from Lydia had no idea. For the last few months she had wandered the world in a curiously asexual state, too focused on her own troubles to register irrelevancies like looks, gender, emotions. Now suddenly here she was, five months into the most nauseous pregnancy in history, sworn off men for the next millennium at the very least, staring across the ward at a man she knew absolutely nothing about and who, more to the point, was probably gay! Giving herself a mental shake, Lydia dragged her eyes back to her notes, trying to cross-reference some lab results on the computer as she filled in the patients' history in her vibrant purple scrawl. Even though she was a registrar, even though she probably wrote the blessed word five times a working day, as she stumbled through the mental block that the spelling of the word 'diarrhoea' eternally produced she found her eyes drifting back to him.

Very good-looking, she mentally reiterated, in a rugged sort of way. Dark curls that needed a cut coiled on the back of a very thick neck, and the set of his wide shoulders made him look more like a rugby player than a neonatal nurse, which, however politically incorrect, begged a question in itself which Lydia answered this time in a nano-second.

Corey Hughes was definitely not gay.

He looked up then, a slightly confused smile crinkling his eyes as he caught her staring. An extremely unbecoming blush whooshed up Lydia's cheeks as he made his way over.

'Everything all right?' he asked, frowning in concern as Lydia fanned her cheeks with a prescription chart.

'Everything's fine. It's just a bit hot in here.'

'Did you want something?'

She was about to say no but, remembering she'd been caught staring, Lydia forced a hasty question. 'I'm trying to get into the computer to see if Patrick's labs are back. I haven't had much luck.'

'Have you used the right password?' Coming round to her side of the desk, Corey peered over her shoulder, leaning forward and tapping away as Lydia sat rigid, staring at the back of his very large hands and trying and failing not to check for a wedding ring.

Absent, as was her pulse for a second as Corey's arm brushed her cheek.

'You're already in,' he said, bemused. 'Did you type in the correct UR number?'

'That must be it.' Lydia flushed even more as Corey tapped away and Patrick's results appeared on the screen. 'They're still not back.'

'They won't be till lunchtime.' Corey frowned. 'I already told you that.'

'So you did.'

He obviously wasn't one for small talk. He made his way back across the ward and resumed whatever it was he had been doing as Lydia stared helplessly at the screen, cheeks flaming, heart pounding, trying to ignore the delicious lingering waft of his after-shave, stunned at the response he'd elicited from her, curiously irritated at her body's rather unloyal response.

She was pregnant, for heaven's sake.

Wasn't that supposed to exalt her to some sort of nun-like status?

Wasn't her libido supposed to vanish with her waist line?

Not that it made a scrap of difference. From the black looks Corey flashed at her every now and then, from the rather terse way he addressed her, this was one relationship that was clearly set to stay professional.

Oh, well, Lydia sighed, pulling out her hair tie at the end of a long and exhausting day, snapping the folders closed and flicking off the light in the cupboard that doubled as her new office.

'I thought you left ages ago.' Corey looked up as she wandered past his office.

'One day in and I'm already behind on the paperwork.'

'Tell me about it.' Corey grimaced, gesturing to his overloaded desk. 'I was supposed to be off at four. Four a.m. more like.'

'You've only got yourself to blame.' When he frowned, Lydia smiled. 'Most NUMs shut themselves in their offices for the best part of the day.'

'Not my style.' Corey shrugged.

'Then stop complaining.'

She was almost smiling and so was Corey, clearly getting her rather dry off-beat humour.

'I've been thinking about your problem and maybe you should come into work a bit earlier,' Corey ventured as Lydia made to go.

'Sorry?' Turning, it was Lydia's turn to frown now.

'In this line of work there will always be paperwork. Why not do only the essentials at the end of the day and leave the rest till the morning, come in half an hour earlier?' When Lydia's frown remained he addressed her as one would a bemused three-year-old. 'Your morning sickness—you said it hits you within half an hour of setting foot in a hospital. If you come in early, you can spend a bit of time acclimatising.'

'Oh!' Lydia blinked a couple of times, the solution so simple she couldn't believe she hadn't already thought of it.

'And you'll have more of the evening to put your feet up and relax.'

'Better and better.' Lydia smiled.

'And I'm sure your husband will be pleased to see a bit more of you.'

She couldn't be sure, the light on his overhead desk didn't allow for an absolute inspection, but for a fleeting second Lydia swore his cheeks darkened.

'There's no husband.' As Lydia swallowed nervously, Corey filled the uncomfortable silence.

'Boyfriend, then.'

'No boyfriend either.' Another nervous swallow and when her voice came it was strangely high. 'When I say no husband, what I meant was—'

Corey put his hand up. 'You really don't need to explain. I mean, I just assumed you had…'

Lydia looked down at her bump, which seemed to be growing like Pinocchio's nose before her eyes, determined to make her feel as fat and as sexless as it was possible to feel, but dragging her eyes up, meeting Corey's full on, her bump seemed to fade into insignificance, the cocktail of hormones fizzing through her bloodstream at that very second definitely not maternal. 'It's a natural assumption,' Lydia said softly. 'So natural, in fact, that I was naïve enough to think it myself. We just got divorced.'

'I'm sorry,' Corey started, but it was Lydia putting her hand up now.

'Don't be.' She gave a small shrug. 'At least, not on my account. I'm saving all the sympathy for this little one.'

Putting a hand up to her stomach, Lydia felt the soft swell of her child beneath and for an awful moment she felt the appalling sting of tears on her lashes, struggled with a bottom lip that seemed to be involuntarily wobbling, before forcing a very brittle, very false smile. ''Night, then.'

''Night.' Either he didn't notice or politely ignored the slight tremor in her voice. Clicking on his pen, he turned to his notes as Lydia scurried through the unit, blinking back tears as she watched the two-by-two world of the neonatal unit, the mothers and fathers hovering by the cots, staring at the fragile miracles they had created, loving each other, leaning on each other. Not for the first time, Lydia wondered how on earth she could do this on her own.

As if on autopilot she washed her hands, made her

way to the only incubator that didn't have a parent beside it, stared at the little scrap of life who really knew what loneliness meant for a moment, before slowly putting her hand in and gently soothing the restless, furrowed brow.

'What have I got to complain about, Patrick?' Lydia said gently, smiling softly as he relaxed under her touch. 'What have I got to complain about?'

CHAPTER TWO

LYDIA hated shopping.

Correction. Lydia loved shopping, adored trying on clothes, slipping her feet into strappy little sandals and pondering her purchase over a well-earned caffe latte.

She merely hated food shopping.

Still, it beat walking into an empty house…

Leaning on a trolley that had a mind of its own, Lydia wandered aimlessly along the aisles, staring in utter bemusement at the rows upon rows of nappies and trying to fathom why it had to be so dammed complicated. Some were in kilos, some were in age, some spoke about softer outer, and stay-dry inners with tiny little teddies that faded when the nappy needed changing. Not for the first time, Lydia felt a surge of panic well inside her.

What on earth was she doing?

How on earth was she supposed to cope with a living, breathing, crying, demanding baby of her very own when she couldn't even decide what type of nappies to purchase? Sure, she dealt with babies every day, handled the most fragile infant with skill and confidence, made life-and-death decisions in the blink of an eye, but, and here was the big one…

At the end of the day she went home!

Picking up speed, she drifted out of the baby aisle, pushing aside her intention to make one purchase a week for the baby. Why change the habits of a lifetime? She always did her Christmas shopping at the last minute and undoubtedly the baby gear would be dealt with in the same vein.

It would all get done in the end.

Humming abstractedly to the piped music, Lydia filled her trolley with a stash of meals for one, before turning into the soft-drink aisle, her lethargic spirits lifting as with a jolt she saw Corey Hughes—or at the least the back of him.

It was becoming a rather familiar response these days. They'd been working alongside each other for a week now and even though the atmosphere between them was still strained, to say the least, even though Lydia thought him a rather arrogant know-all, her body simply refused to listen, insisting upon darkening her face with a blush and sending her heart rate into overdrive every time she glimpsed him!

Disappointingly, though, one arm was rather protectively around an incredibly tiny, incredibly pretty woman, while with the other he struggled to contain the most appallingly behaved child in the history of the world.

For a second Lydia considered making a hasty U-turn, darting back to the relative safety of the nappy section, but the thought of Corey catching her making a rapid retreat, of seeing the effect he was having on her, was enough incentive to beat back her blush. She sauntered in what she hoped was a casual way along the aisle, pretending to concentrate on the soft drinks, practising a casual hello and smile in her head as she worked her way nearer, then realising as she edged closer that she needn't have bothered.

Corey was so engrossed in cartons of orange juice

that, had she stripped off and congaed naked behind her shopping trolley, she doubted he'd have even looked up. Instead of disciplining his appalling child, instead of forcing the squealing, tantrum-throwing toddler back into its stroller, his deep loud voice droned on and on about the merits of home brands as opposed to named ones, to check for any special offers and, of course, to always look at the contents. It might look like a bargain but if there were only four hundred mls in the container...

It was at that point that Lydia questioned the merits of first impressions.

That sexy, rugged, good-looking guy evaporated there and then. To see him at his domestic worst truly pulled the wool from Lydia's eyes and she was eternally grateful for it.

She hated meanness in men, hated it more than anything in the world, well, except for adultery, but that wasn't the issue here. She could just imagine him in the loo-roll section—he'd probably whip out a calculator and work out the sheets per roll and the benefits of two- as opposed to four-ply.

'Lydia!'

Truly caught, she had no choice but to smile, but due to her sudden insight there was no trace of awkwardness. 'So you're a late-night shopping addict, too.'

'Absolutely.' Corey smiled warmly. 'Fewer people...'

'More chance of spotting a bargain.' Lydia muttered. Glancing down at her own trolley, she realised how empty her statement sounded. For all her determination, for all her self-conditioning and occasional attempts, somehow cooking chicken massala from scratch seemed so dammed complicated and, perhaps more to the point, when flour and coconut milk weren't staples of your larder, so damned expensive.

She was saving money really!

Still for tight gits like Corey, her trolley probably did look rather extravagant!

'This is Adele.' Corey gave a wide smile as Lydia nodded politely. 'And this is Bailey.'

Bailey didn't look up. He was too busy pulling orange juice off the shelves and creating chaos to care about introductions as Adele stood silently, her pretty face almost surly as she eyed Lydia, clearly uncomfortable at the intrusion.

'Best get on.' Lydia smiled, moving gratefully into aisle four and immersing herself in two-minute noodles.

They met again at the checkout, Lydia blushing to her roots as Corey counted out the notes to the cashier, checked and rechecked his change with the unfortunate Adele while Bailey helped himself to a large slab of chocolate from the display stand.

'Poor woman,' Lydia muttered to the checkout girl as finally they moved off.

'Oh, I don't know…' The checkout girl looked dreamily over her shoulder as the trio departed, didn't even offer Lydia the mandatory 'How are you tonight?' 'I think he's kind of cute.'

This was the bit she hated—unloading the groceries from the boot of the car, lugging them up the garden path and heaving the bags into a dark, empty house.

No one to come out and offer to help, no one to moan she'd forgotten to get coffee-beans…

No one, full stop.

Not that she minded her own company. When Gavin had still lived there, invariably he'd be away on some course or interstate on some business trip—at least, that's what he'd said he'd been doing, Lydia thought darkly, filling her freezer with her purchases. She hadn't minded a bit—in fact, she'd actually enjoyed it in many ways. Having beans on toast, or just toast for dinner, even taking the said toast into bed and curling up with a good book.

Gavin had hated that.

Come to think of it, Gavin had hated a lot of things in the last few months of their marriage.

Slamming the freezer door closed, Lydia pulled a couple of slices of bread out of the pantry and loaded them into the toaster.

Toast, a good book and bed.

What more could a girl want?

'I've saved you a ticket.'

Frowning into the telephone that seemed to be permanently glued to her ear these days, Lydia looked up.

'For what?'

'The special care unit Christmas fundraising ball. It's held every year at the beginning of December and it usually turns out to be a great night.'

'No, don't put me back on hold,' Lydia yelped as finally a human voice responded, but as the music droned on Lydia settled back for the long haul, digging in her pocket for a proverbial ten-dollar note then baulking as she eyed the gold-rimmed ticket more closely. 'Two hundred dollars!'

'It's a black-tie do.' Corey shrugged. 'And the money goes to a good cause.'

'It's a bloody rip-off.''

He thought she was joking. Looking up, she watched him laugh, waiting for her to pull out her cheque book, to sign herself up for taxi fare both ways and a maternity ballgown that would make the ticket price pale into comparison, but for the first time in her adult life Lydia couldn't do it, couldn't write a cheque for the sake of it, couldn't rob Peter to pay Paul. Suddenly money mattered when it never had before,

'I'll let you know.' Frowning into the telephone, Lydia turned away but still he persisted.

'You're not working.' Corey grinned. 'I've checked, so there's no excuse.'

'How about this for an excuse?' Swinging her chair around, Lydia met him face on, her cheeks burning with embarrassment at having to admit the appalling truth, her voice too harsh, too sharp as she choked on the pride she was being forced to swallow yet again. 'For someone who's so up on the price of orange juice, for someone who checks their change three times before moving off from the checkout, you're terribly careless where other people's money is concerned.

'Did it never occur to you that just because I'm a registrar, just because I'm supposedly affluent and raking it in—maybe that isn't the case?' She watched his eyes widen, watched as he attempted to beg to differ, but Lydia was on a roll now. 'Would you be quite so accepting if your wife strolled home with a two-hundred-dollar ticket in her hand?'

'I don't have a wife.' Corey shrugged.

'Well, girlfriend, then,' Lydia snapped. 'The poor woman's received a five-minute lecture into the variances of orange juice prices and she has to show you her cashier's receipt, yet you don't bat an eyelid when it's a co-worker's money you're spending!'

Suddenly the temperature seemed to have dropped, suddenly the usually stifling nurses' station seemed to be taking on arctic proportions. As she watched his face darken Lydia knew she'd gone way too far. 'I'm sorry,' she said quickly. 'That was way below the belt.'

'It was,' Corey agreed grimly, and Lydia shifted uncomfortably as he carried on talking. 'Adele's not my wife and neither do I have a girlfriend or a son.' He watched her frown, watched her squirm for an uncomfortable second before continuing.

'Adele's my sister, Bailey's my nephew, and for your information I personally couldn't give a damn about the price of orange juice, but given the fact my sister was involved in a car accident two years ago and she has changed from an eloquent, educated woman into someone with the personality of an errant teenager, it seems rather more fitting to show her that ten dollars can be spent on staples like bread and orange juice rather than a basket full of crisps and bubble gum or cheap wine and cigarettes.'

'I'm sorry.' Lydia's voice was a faint whisper. 'I'm so very sorry.'

'Not as sorry as I am,' Corey responded curtly, and picking up his stethoscope he shot her a black look before stalking off to his office. She was vaguely aware of a voice on the telephone line, vaguely aware of someone asking how they could help, but mumbling her apologies Lydia hung up the telephone, appalled at what she had done and desperate if not to put things right exactly to at least make some sort of amends.

Knocking on his office door, she neither expected nor received a response. Pushing the door open, she stood for a hesitant moment watching as Corey scribbled furiously on the paperwork in front of him, determinedly not looking up. Lydia rather less determinedly moved the pile of folders herself this time and, after making sure the door was firmly closed behind her, tentatively sat down.

'I'm sorry.'

'So you said.'

'I'd like to explain something—'

'There's really no need,' Corey cut in, fixing her with a most withering glare.

'But there is.' Dragging her eyes down, Lydia went to fiddle with the solid gold band around her wedding finger, as she did when she was nervous, but like everything else familiar to her it wasn't there. 'What I said out there was wrong. Whether Adele is your sister, wife or girlfriend, I had absolutely no right to pass judgement on you, no right to infer you were mean.' She was tying her fingers in knots now. 'Which you're not, of course, but even if you were, even if you do care about the price of loo rolls...'

'We were in the soft-drink section,' Corey pointed out, and if she'd looked up at that point she'd have been rewarded with a ghost of a smile. 'Where do loo rolls come into it?'

'They don't.' Her eyes did meet his then, briefly, awkwardly and she immediately pulled them away. 'What I'm trying to say is that I was way out of line.'

'You were,' Corey agreed, but more gently this time. 'But I was probably being overly sensitive.' Those massive shoulders moved downwards as he gave a ragged sigh, and Lydia saw the lines of concern grooved around his eyes. 'There's a lot going on there.'

'With Adele?'

Corey nodded. 'She was a lawyer. Hard to believe it now, but she was the epitome of sophistication. Somehow she and Luke made it all look so damn easy.'

'Luke's her husband?' Lydia checked, wincing when Corey continued.

'Was. He was killed in the car accident. Adele was in a coma for six weeks. We were so close to making that awful decision—to discontinue treatment. She was so sick and there really seemed no hope.'

'But look how well she's done,' Lydia said optimistically, her voice trailing off as Corey shook his head.

'She suffered massive brain injuries—she's got frontal lobe damage, which means no inhibitions and no responsibility for her actions. Sometimes I wonder if we did the right thing.' Strained eyes met hers. 'You've seen Bailey. No doubt you think the kid needs a good smack, to be disciplined...'

Lydia shook her head, but her blush gave her away.

'You wouldn't be alone,' Corey said sadly. 'Bailey

was in the accident as well. He's undergoing a load of tests, they're not sure if he suffered brain damage himself or if he's got attention deficit disorder. His paediatrician has even started to suggest autism.'

'What do you think?' Lydia asked, hearing the doubt in his voice.

'I think it's a rather more basic problem.'

'Such as?' The room was deathly quiet now and it took an age for him to answer.

'Neglect,' Corey said finally. 'I've made so many excuses for her, rushed over there to clean up before the social worker comes, filled up her fridge with healthy food. I go round every night or morning and bath him, cut his toenails, clean his ears, all the things Adele wouldn't even think of doing, but...'

'It's not enough?' Lydia ventured, watching as Corey shook his head sadly.

'I don't know what to do,' Corey admitted. 'So if I jumped down your throat out there, it was with reason.'

'You had every right to jump down my throat,' Lydia said softly. 'Even without what you've just told me. I know I can be harsh sometimes, know I can come across as rude. In fact, it's becoming rather a habit.' Tears were appallingly close now, but she blinked them away, picking instead at an imaginary piece of fluff on her theatre blues. 'I seem to be eternally putting my foot in it these days, snapping people's heads off, saying the wrong thing...'

'You've got a lot on your mind.'

'I know,' Lydia admitted, 'but so do you and yet you still manage to come to work with a smile. It would be nice to manage a simple greeting without messing things up.'

'I think you're being a bit harsh on yourself. I haven't had any complaints from the staff and the parents seem to like you.'

'Because I talk to them about medicine,' Lydia snapped, and then bit it back, shrugging her shoulders helplessly at her own abrasiveness. 'Six months ago I was an entirely different person.' She gestured to the window, and they stared out through the half-open blinds for a second or two before Lydia carried on talking. 'See Jo there, chatting away while she works, laughing at something someone's said? Well, that was *me*. I knew all the staff, and I don't mean just their names, I knew what was happening in their lives.'

'You've only been here a couple of weeks,' Corey pointed out, but Lydia shook her head.

'I'm a fast learner. I get on with people, or at least I used to.' Green eyes were staring at her now, the anger gone from them. But Lydia knew he deserved an explanation and, perhaps more pointedly, she wanted to tell him her story, though why she couldn't quite fathom.

'I thought we had a good marriage. Gavin was a pharmacologist working for a big US drug company. He was away a lot, but I didn't mind.' Corey didn't say anything, just headed for the inevitable kettle, making a cup of tea as she carried on talking. Lydia was infinitely grateful for the reprieve from his gaze as she told her difficult tale. 'He was involved in drug trials on my old ward. It was terribly complicated and meant he was there a lot.'

'You didn't mind?' It was the first time Corey had

spoken, his hand hovering over the sugar bowl but his back still to her. 'Seeing him at work every day?'

'Not in the slightest. I mean, we were so busy there wasn't exactly time for social chit-chat, at least not on my part.' She watched him spoon the sugar into her mug, watched as it passed the one mark and went to two, didn't even think to stop him as a third sugar hit was ladled into the brew. Accepting the sickly offer, she took a sip, glad of the sweet warmth before she continued. 'You asked where the loo rolls came into things.' A hollow laugh filled the room. 'Suddenly we were rowing about everything, even down to loo rolls, but whenever I pushed, whenever I asked what was wrong, I got the same response: "I'm just tired." I knew that wasn't it, knew there must be something else...' Her voice trailed off and Corey spoke for her.

'He was having an affair?'

'Of course.' She watched as he blinked in surprise at her openness, even managed a wry smile of her own as she found her voice again. 'But that's not the best bit. As I said, I knew there was something wrong and finally Gavin came up with an answer. He wanted a baby, figured that now we were in our thirties it wasn't such an unreasonable request.'

'You didn't want children?'

Lydia shook her head. 'No. When people asked, I always qualified that with "not for ages", but the honest answer is I really didn't want to have a child. I love my work, loved my husband, it was truly enough for me.'

'But not for Gavin?'

'Seemingly not. He knew I didn't want children

and with hindsight I guess it was the one thing he could hang on me, apportion blame to. I guess he didn't know me well enough.' Tired, confused eyes met his. 'I came off the Pill.' Her voice dropped so low it was barely audible. 'Figured I was being self-ish. After all, it was hardly an unreasonable request—we'd been married five years, for heaven's sake. I should have held my ground.'

Realising she'd lost him, Lydia gave a tired shrug.

'It turned out he never wanted a baby either. It was just an excuse, an excuse to dust away the rows, to explain the sudden lethargy and the problems we sup-posedly had. Gavin no more wanted a child than I did. I found out he was sleeping with one of the nurses on my ward.'

'Oh, no.' She heard the genuine shock in Corey's voice but it bought no comfort. Lydia was far too used to being the centre of gossip, way too used to the incredulous reaction to the news.

'Oh, yes! He'd been sleeping with Marcia for three months, and the worst part was I thought she was my friend.' Her eyes screwed closed for a second. 'She was actually my best friend. I thought we were really close, I'm not one for opening up…'

'I'd never have guessed.'

His dry comment even forced a tiny smile but it didn't last long as Lydia continued her painful tale. 'I'd even confided in her about our problems, told her I was thinking of coming off the Pill…' Gripping her fists tightly in her lap, Lydia took a deep breath before continuing. 'I know it was a one-off, know most peo-ple don't behave like that, would be appalled by

Marcia's behaviour, but I simply don't know how to respond any more, I don't know who I can trust.'

'You can trust me.' The directness of his statement caught her unawares, dragged her out of her introspection, enough to at least meet his eyes. 'I know I'm no compensation for an errant husband and a lousy best friend, but I can be a good ally when needed.'

Lydia nodded. 'When you asked for the money—'

'Forget it,' Corey said. 'It was my turn to be insensitive, my turn to make stupid assumptions. You're right. Because you're a registrar, because you've got fabulous nails and immaculate hair, I assumed you were loaded.'

'Immaculate hair.' Lydia gave an incredulous laugh. 'It's all over the place.'

'So is Nicole Kidman's,' Corey pointed out.

Lydia gave a dry laugh. 'Ah, but mine's naturally chaotic.' Peering down at her hands, Lydia stared at her nails.

And very nice they looked, too! But only because she'd given up biting them, only because she'd awarded herself a weekly home manicure as a treat for not chewing the blessed things.

'As seemingly unplanned as this baby was, I had at least worked out the basics.' Her eyes were still focused on her nails, the uncomfortable subject of money not really allowing for eye contact. 'I was due long service leave, I'd worked at Bayside for years, I had more sick days and annual leave owing than anyone I've ever met, the pay office was always ringing and insisting I take a break…'

'But the roster never accommodated,' Corey filled in wisely, and Lydia nodded.

'I could have taken close to a year off on full pay, bar shift allowance, but at the end of the day I couldn't do it, couldn't stay there another minute, with everyone knowing my business, everyone feeling sorry for me.'

'Did Marcia leave?'

'Why would she?' Lydia responded, surprisingly without bitterness. 'When I was more than ready to?

'So now I'm having the baby Gavin insisted he wanted but evidently didn't and facing three months off with no maternity leave pay. And as I bought Gavin out, I've now got a mortgage that would feed a third world country.'

'You can make him pay,' Corey ventured, but watching her stiffen he changed track. 'Sorry, wrong choice of words. What I'm trying to say—'

'I know,' Lydia gulped. 'And you're right, I could make him pay: drag him through the children's court for alimony and child support. But I'm not going to do it, Corey, because guess what? I neither want nor need his help. He signed himself out of this marriage when he slept with Marcia, and for a guy who's so wrapped up in saving lives with his bloody drug trials, he couldn't even raise a smile when he found out I was pregnant. So if you think I'm going to run to him with a begging bowl...' She stopped, realising her anger, however merited, was misdirected. 'I'd love to go to the ball, love to dig in my bag and sign a cheque, but the simple truth is I can't.' Lydia gave a dry smile 'Have you seen the price of nappies?''

'Wait till they're weaned and hit the orange juice!'

She would have laughed but tears had started. Corey pushed a box of tissues over the desk and when she couldn't quite reach it he came around, wrapping her in his arms as if she were a rugby ball, letting her cry as if it was the most natural thing in the world, not remotely embarrassed as he held her and wiped rivers of mascara from her cheeks.

And somewhere in mid-gulp, somewhere between another tissue and a glass of water, those arms that were holding her didn't feel quite so comforting any more, the aftershave filling her nostrils not quite so reassuring…

Panicky and out of control would be a rather more apt description, and for the first time in months it had nothing to do with an errant husband and a baby that hadn't been on the agenda.

For the first time in months it had everything nice to do with being a woman.

CHAPTER THREE

'SO THIS is where you've been hiding?'

Jumping slightly as Corey plonked himself on the seat beside her, Lydia suddenly took great interest in the hospital canteen's chocolate chip muffin.

'I'm hardly in a position to hide.' Lydia smiled. 'I just caught sight of myself in the full-length windows so I'm cheering myself up with a bit of cake, which probably makes no sense at all...' She was waffling now, badly. Corey Hughes had that effect on her for some strange reason.

Maybe strange wasn't the right word, Lydia mused, pulling her muffin apart and searching for the rather scarce chocolate chips. In fact, the effect Corey had on her was probably considered entirely normal. After all, men and women definitely weren't created equal and the major physiological reaction Corey triggered in her was a natural biological response—a phenomenon as old as time itself! Since their near-argument, since they'd glimpsed each other's lives, opened up a touch, Lydia was blushing like a teenager at every turn, glancing at the nursing roster with way more than a passing interest and trying to fathom how a newly divorced, rather pregnant, born-again virgin could even be contemplating falling in lust all over again!

'How come you're not in the senior doctors'

lounge?' Corey grinned. 'I hear they serve muffins on a plate there, as opposed to wrapped in cling film.'

'They do,' Lydia quipped. 'And I have to admit that entering the hallowed ground of the senior doctors' lounge for the first time was pretty exciting—at least, for the first five minutes.'

'Not the most scintillating company, then?'

'Not for someone like me.' When Corey gave a small, quizzical frown, Lydia elaborated. 'I'm a confirmed people-watcher, and what better place to do it than at a hospital?'

'I'm not with you.'

'Well, one has such a head start here,' Lydia explained. 'After all, they're either a member of staff, a patient or a visitor—it only takes a moment or two to work out which.' When Corey's expression remained perplexed, she explained further. 'I like working people out. Look...' She pointed to an elderly couple wandering along the corridor. 'Dressed in their Sunday best, so they could be visitors, but see how she's holding an envelope. Well, from that I'd guess that they've got an outpatients appointment.'

'Who's the patient?' Corey asked, smiling as he played along.

'He is,' Lydia said firmly. 'Don't you just love how old people dress up to go to see the doctor? I think it's just so adorable. See how she's walking ahead, sort of hurrying him along, and she's got a really brave strong expression on her face, whereas he looks as if at any moment he'll turn tail and run. I expect he doesn't want to hear the news if it's bad.'

'What news?'

'About his prostate. They've just turned down to

Four West and that's where the urology outpatients clinic is being held.'

'How do you know all this?' Corey asked, bemused.

'I read the signs.'

'Do you, now?'

Whoops!

If ever Lydia had wished she could erase a comment, it was now. Unless she'd got things seriously wrong, unless she was very much mistaken, from the blush working its way up her cheeks, from the rapid pulse flickering in her neck and the sudden intimate smile Corey was imparting, written in neon and pulsing above them was a rather large sign, with cupid's arrows and rather tasteless pink hearts to boot!

'That muffin looks good.' His voice seemed to be coming at her through a fog. 'I might even go and get one for myself.'

'You should.' Lydia smiled, while trying to remember how her mouth worked. 'But I'm afraid you're going to have to take over the ''watch'', I have to get going.'

'I think I'll give it a miss, thanks.' His eyes held hers for the longest time. 'I prefer to get the facts first, get to know people a bit and then make up my mind.'

It was totally in line with the conversation, every last word was appropriate, so why did Lydia feel her blush coming back for an encorc? Why in the crowded hospital coffee-shop did it suddenly feel as if there were only the two of them?

'I really ought to go.' Her voice was a mere croak.

'I'm supposed to be meeting Dr Reece in a few minutes.'

'About Patrick?'

The invisible neon sign above them vanished in an invisible puff of smoke as they reverted to the far safer topic of work.

'They didn't seem too happy with his latest results; they want to go over a few things.'

'You'll let me know how things go?' Corey checked as Lydia stood up, automatically checking her pager was on as she did so.

'Of course.' Lydia smiled. 'Page me if you need me.'

'This is Dr Verhagh.' Pushing forward an anxious-looking woman in a wheelchair, Jo smiled warmly as she handed Lydia a thick pile of notes. 'Dr Verhagh will probably be at the delivery, but if not, you can expect to see her when your baby comes to the special care unit.'

'Lydia,' Lydia introduced herself, shaking the nervous woman's hand warmly. The meeting with Dr Reece, the cardiac surgeon, had been rather grim and she'd been hoping to discuss things with Corey, but clearly it would have to wait. 'Dr Hamilton, your obstetrician, rang me this morning and said you'd be coming in for a look around. It's Meredith Clarke, isn't it?'

Lydia had been there five weeks now and was used to seeing parents being given the guided tour. It was the same as at her old job. What was different, however, was that as a registrar it was now Lydia talking to the parents, making decisions with the obstetricians, and she revelled in it, enjoying the responsibility her new role brought while never taking it lightly.

But it wasn't just the medical side of her job she was enjoying now, Lydia realised as she smiled at Jo and Meredith. Since her talk with Corey things had been easier. The fact he knew her problems had actually helped. OK, she wasn't the social butterfly of the unit, people didn't rush to have a coffee with her and she didn't exactly light up the room when she walked in, but at least she was able to string together a bit of small talk now, pass a few pleasantries and manage a natural smile.

'I'm just showing her around,' Jo added quietly. 'Meredith's just been told that her baby will be born in the next week or so. I think she might have a few questions for you.'

'That's fine,' Lydia murmured before addressing the woman. 'It's a bit offputting at first,' Lydia ventured, as a loud alarm blipped, causing Meredith to start, 'but you'll soon get used to it. Most of the time, when an alarm goes off it merely means that the baby's moved and dislodged a probe. It's really not as alarming as it first appears.'

Meredith nodded, but didn't look particularly convinced. Casting an anxious look around, Meredith's eyes widened as she saw the tiny babies, the acres of tubing and equipment and the sheer high volume of the unit. Her hand reached down to her swollen stomach, unthinkingly massaging the child within as she finally turned and smiled bravely back at the doctor.

'When are you due?' Lydia asked, taking over the

wheelchair handles as Jo gratefully bobbed back to her charge.

'Well, it wasn't supposed to be until January but my obstetrician told me that I can expect to deliver in the next few days. Apparently my placenta isn't working properly and the baby has IGU...' Her voice faltered at the unfamiliar medical terminology and Lydia stepped in.

'IUGR,' Lydia said. 'I'll write it down for you. It stands for intra-uterine growth retardation.'

'That's it,' Meredith agreed, relaxing somewhat as Lydia steered the wheelchair away from the shop floor and to the parents' coffee-room.

'IUGR means the baby isn't growing in your womb as well as we'd expect and from what your obstetrician told me when I spoke with him, it would seem that your placenta isn't working as well as it should.'

'But why?' Meredith asked. 'I've done everything right. I've been eating well, too well my husband says, so why are things going wrong now?'

'Sometimes these things just happen, Meredith, and it isn't anyone's fault.' Lydia gave a sympathetic smile. She'd heard this question more times than she could remember and wished she could give a better answer.

'Can I get you a drink?'

Meredith shook her head. 'I'm fine, thanks, just a bit...'

'Overwhelmed?' Lydia suggested. 'I know how scary this must all seem to you, but in some cases, particularly like yours, the baby really is better born. I've discussed your case at length with your obstetrician and we both agree that this little one is best born sooner rather than later, but we're going to try and hold off for a few more days. Once the baby's here we can give it all the nutrients it's been missing out *in utero* and hopefully he or she will do really well. Do you know what you're having?''

'No, I wanted it to be a surprise.'

Lydia was flicking through the notes as she spoke, reading the ultrasound reports and the latest cord studies and looking at the graph the obstetrician had duly plotted. The baby was indeed small, but not alarmingly so, and although early, thirty weeks gestation was almost routine in the special care unit, what was of more concern was its failure to progress in the last couple of weeks or so. 'So your expected delivery date was...' Lydia scanned the notes but Meredith beat her to it.

'January the twenty-second.' She didn't notice Lydia's pen hover over the page, didn't notice the sudden tension in the doctor's shoulders. 'I'm trying to understand what everyone's saying. I mean, everyone's being really nice but, however nicely it's put, I know in my heart that it's too soon.' Tears were starting now. 'I'm just so scared and if the baby's so bad why don't they just deliver me now? Why keep me waiting? I just don't understand!'

Lydia was used to dealing with anxious relatives, used to reassuring them, even used to dashing dreams, but January the twenty-second was a familiar date for Lydia also, the date her own baby was due, and she realised then how hollow her platitudes would sound, how truly terrified she'd be herself if she were in Meredith's shoes.

She would have loved to inch herself off the sofa,

but heave was perhaps a more apt description and crossing the short distance between them Lydia wrapped her arms around the woman. 'We're going to do our very best for your baby, Meredith, I can promise you that. What I can't promise is that everything is going to be fine. I can only assure you that the decision hasn't been taken lightly to deliver your baby. Dr Hamilton is trying to keep the baby inside you for a few more days to nudge it well over the thirty-week mark. It might only sound like a few days, but every day your baby is inside you, even if it isn't putting on weight, its little lungs will be maturing and statistically your baby has a chance of doing better if we can hold off for just a little longer.'

'What if something happens, though? I mean before then.'

'Dr Hamilton and the midwives are watching the baby very closely on the antenatal ward. The ultrasounds you're having and the regular monitoring on the CTG enable us to see how the baby is coping. As soon as we feel it's being compromised, we'll deliver you.'

'I just feel so helpless.'

Lydia gave a dry smile. 'That's pregnancy for you. But you're really not helpless, Meredith. Rest and eat and try not to get too worked up—that will give your baby the best chance of staying put for just a little bit longer. However much we rely on all the equipment, mums are still the best judges as to how things are progressing.' She watched Meredith frown. 'Are you keeping a kick chart?'

Meredith gave a small shrug. 'I am, but I have to

admit I thought it was just something the nurses were giving me to do to humour me.'

'Not at all.' Lydia shook her head firmly. 'Believe me, the day you say the kicks are slowing or starting to tail off is going to be the day Dr Hamilton delivers. It's teamwork here, Meredith. We've all got the same goal: a healthy baby for you take to home.'

'Absolutely.'

Lydia jumped slightly when she heard the all-too-familiar voice of Corey. 'The antenatal ward just rang, Meredith. It seems we've kept you out partying too long.'

His humour bought a smile to Meredith's pale lips. 'I've broken my curfew, have I?'

'Something like that.' Corey nodded. 'Geoff the porter's here to wheel you back down. Have all your questions been answered?'

'They have now.' She gave a shy smile in Lydia's direction. 'You've been very understanding.'

'We'll see you again soon.' Lydia smiled.

'Not too soon, I hope,' Meredith sighed as Geoff came in and started to wheel her off. 'But if it is…'

'Then we'll deal with it,' Lydia said firmly, but her eyes were kind.

Alone with Corey, suddenly Lydia felt uncomfortable, not unpleasantly so, more in a gauche teenager kind of way.

'You were very good with her.'

'I wasn't at first,' Lydia admitted. 'I think I blinded her with science for a while there…' He watched as she ran a worried hand across her forehead. 'We've got the same delivery date and it came as a bit of a shock. I mean, I know it shouldn't, half the babies on the unit are due around the time of mine, but hearing the exact same date kind of forced me into her shoes.'

'Thirty weeks sound so big to us here,' Corey mused. 'But it's going to be scary for her. For you, too,' he added.

'For me?' Lydia frowned. 'Why?'

'Just wait and see, huh? But if you need an ear at any point, you can bend mine. Anyway, changing the subject...' He gestured for her to follow and Lydia walked behind him to his office still frowning to herself, wondering what on earth he'd meant. But her personal questions were put on hold as Corey closed the door and put on his grim management face.

'Patrick's mother has been in touch.'

'When did this happen?' Lydia asked, helping herself to a seat while Corey stood.

'Just. She rang the ward. I would have paged you but I knew you were in a meeting and didn't want her to ring off while I put her on hold. I thought—'

'That's fine,' Lydia interrupted. She was no prima donna and in truth she knew that Corey would probably have dealt with the situation as well as if not better than herself. 'Is she coming in?'

Corey shook his head. 'She just wanted to know how he was doing.'

'How was she?'

'Very tearful, of course, but she said she was trying to get herself sorted, to straighten herself out. She's trying to pluck up the courage to come and see him.' As Lydia opened her mouth to speak, Corey's eyes met hers. 'I told her there may not be time to wait, that Patrick was very sick and if she wanted to see her son then it should be sooner rather than later.'

'Do you think she understood?'

'No,' Corey said simply. 'And rather more worrying is that she now doesn't want him to be operated on. Jenny isn't sure if she wants him to undergo surgery.'

Lydia let out a long breath, the legal implications of his mother's refusal a worrying turn of events. 'That's not necessarily her decision to make, Corey. We need to let Legal know, we need to—'

'I know all that,' Corey broke in. 'And I will get onto it. But I think I should go over things with Jenny first; reiterate the facts. I don't think we should write her off just yet. She's his mother and, given time, I'm sure she'll come around.' Even though his tone was impassive, even though he was still in his NUM mode, a worried frown puckered Lydia's brow.

Emotions had to be left at the door of the special care unit.

Sure, the staff got involved, worked closely with the parents, rode the roller-coaster of emotions along with them, but to be there and survive, a certain personality was called for. Someone who could detach themselves, see the bigger picture perhaps, but wear blinkers when necessary—a vital tool if you wanted to survive. And Corey, for whatever reason, wasn't playing by the rules.

'Patrick doesn't have time,' Lydia said firmly, wearing her stern doctor's face. 'I've just come from a meeting with Dr Reece. I was on my way to talk to you before I got waylaid with Meredith.'

'And?'

'They're talking about bringing his operation forward.'

'He's too weak.' Corey shook his head. 'Dr Reece wanted to wait till he was three months, or at least till he'd put on a bit more weight.'

'That was the ideal,' Lydia agreed crisply, and there was an air of authority to her voice, determined to keep this meeting businesslike. 'But there's been nothing ideal about Patrick's progress. He needs to have the surgery for there to be any hope of survival.' She let the news sink in for a moment before continuing. 'Legal needs to be notified of the latest developments immediately and we'll have to take it from there.'

'Maybe I could go round there.' Corey ignored her shaking head. 'Go to the rehab unit and talk to her, take some photos.'

'That's the social worker's job,' Lydia pointed out. 'And Jenny has enough to deal with, without you rocking up there and piling on the guilt.'

'That's not my intention,' Corey flared. 'Patrick's problems aren't all her fault. He's got Down's syndrome, the bloods came back confirming the fact.'

'I'm aware of that, but it doesn't account for all his difficulties, and with the best will in the world you can't dismiss the fact that a cask of wine a day or the best part of a bottle of Scotch contributed to Patrick's problems. You can't get too involved, Corey.'

'I'm not.' Corey answered, but the disbelieving look in Lydia's eyes clearly irritated him and he stared back defiantly. 'I'm the nurse unit manager, for goodness' sake. I've been doing this for years. I, more than anyone, know the perils of getting too close.'

'Then hand it over to Legal, Corey.' She knew she was coming across as harsh but it was a calculated move. For whatever reason, Corey was in way too deep and Lydia had to make him pull back. 'Just because she's his mother, it doesn't mean she's the best person to look after him.' For a second she thought she'd gone too far, saw the grim set of his mouth, and Lydia realised she'd touched a raw nerve. Realisation started to dawn and even though she knew her question was personal, Lydia decided in a flash it was merited. 'You're not comparing Patrick to Bailey?'

'Don't be ridiculous.' Corey's voice had a warning note in it not to push, which Lydia pointedly ignored.

'Because if you are, Corey, then you're heading into dangerous territory. You need to pull back from Patrick. 'She chewed on the edge of her pen for a moment, wondering how to play this. Corey was simply the best NUM she'd worked with; he, ran the unit impeccably, watched out for this type of situation in his staff.

But who was watching out for him?

'You need to hand this over to the appropriate departments and pull back a touch from Patrick.' Defiant eyes met hers but she held his gaze. 'I'm on a couple of days off after this shift but when I come back I expect this all to have been sorted and handed over. Think about what I'm saying Corey,' Lydia said softly, but there was no mistaking the seriousness behind her words, 'because otherwise I'll do it for you.'

For a moment his face darkened and Lydia braced herself, sure a row was about to ensue. But not for the first time Corey utterly disarmed her, flooring her with one of his easy smiles and giving a dismissive shrug.

'Fine,' he said, as Lydia blinked in surprise, staring back at him doubtfully. 'I'll think about what you've said and I'll hand it all over, but you're reading too much into it, Lydia.

'Anyway, onto more pleasant things...' Digging in his pocket, he suddenly couldn't quite catch her eye.

'Wh-what's this?' she stammered, as a rather familiar-looking gold ticket was pressed into her hands.

'A ticket to the ball, or at least it was the last time I looked.'

'I can see that,' Lydia said, cheeks scorching as she stared at the beastly ticket, but this time she read it more closely. A sumptuous four-course Christmas dinner, followed by a rather impressive raffle and a night of dancing sounded divine, and even though it was the last thing on earth she could really afford, Lydia knew deep down she had no choice but to go.

That as a registrar she really had no choice but to attend.

'OK.' She smiled, knowing she was beaten. 'You win! My cheque book's in my bag. I won't be a moment...' Turning to go, she frowned as Corey called her back.

'I'm not trying to sell you a ticket, Lydia.' This time it was Corey looking slightly unsure, this time it was Corey looking everywhere but at her. 'I'm asking you to come with me.'

'With you?'

'I bought two tickets...'

'No,' Lydia wailed. 'I'm not a charity case. I know how much they cost and you certainly don't have to fork out for me—that wasn't what I was after.'

'Hell, you don't make things easy, do you?' He gave an awkward smile. 'I'm asking you out, Lydia.'

'Out?'

'On a date.'

'A date?' Her cheeks were positively purple now. 'I've forgotten what a date is.'

'It's been that long, huh?'

'Years,' Lydia admitted, staring down at the ticket.

'Look, it's not for a couple of weeks yet—that gives you plenty of time to come up with a better reason to say no, but for now, why not just say yes?' When still she didn't respond he pushed harder. 'At least think about it?'

'Corey, this is too much…'

'It's all for a good cause,' Corey pointed out, but Lydia shook her head.

'I'm not just talking about the price of the ticket, Corey.' She dragged her eyes up to him, forced herself to look at him, and once she was there found it wasn't actually that hard. Corey was certainly pleasing on the eye and even more endearingly his awkwardness as he awaited her response was as palpable as her own. 'I'm pregnant, for goodness' sake.'

'Are you?' The feigned surprise in his voice made Lydia smile.

'Which doesn't exactly equate with dating.'

'Why not?'

Lydia shrugged helplessly. 'It just doesn't. I'm supposed to be at home knitting or something and thinking all sorts of mumsy thoughts…'

'Such as?'

'What colour to paint the nursery, what I'm going to call it.'

'It?'

'The baby,' Lydia wailed, but a grin was parting her lips now.

'Lemon,' Corey quipped. 'If you don't know what you're having, then lemon's the safest bet, and I've got a name book in the office you can read on your coffee-break. And as for knitting, why on earth would you bother when you can go to shops and buy one?'

'I can't knit,' Lydia admitted.

'Thank God for that,' Corey said. 'Somehow I can't quite picture you in a rocking chair with a pair of knitting needles.'

'How do you picture me?' They were both heading into dangerous territory now, the air throbbing with sexual tension as the gentle hums of flirting took over.

'Draped in black velvet, very high heels that you won't find in a maternity shop and long, long earrings.'

Still she didn't give her answer.

'I like you, Lydia. I have since the day you burst onto the ward, all prickly and formal. And I'm sorry if this isn't what you want to hear, but when I found out you were divorced I was hard pushed to say I was sorry. In fact, it cheered me up no end.' She opened her mouth to speak but Corey overrode her. 'I like you, Lydia, and I'm pretty sure that you like me.'

'I do,' Lydia admitted. 'And that's probably why I flared up so much about the supermarket incident.' She saw him frown, realised he had no idea where she was leading. 'I *was* disappointed when I thought Adele was your wife...' Worried eyes met his. 'I'm pregnant,' she said again, very, very slowly, so she could be absolutely sure he understood, that he didn't just think she'd missed out on doing her sit-ups for the last decade, that he really realised there was a baby growing inside her which in a few short weeks would be making an entrance.

'You're gorgeous, Lydia,' Corey said equally slowly. 'And you also happen to be pregnant. Now, for the third and final time, will you come to the ball with me?'

She went to stare back at the ticket but suddenly her eyes wouldn't move. Instead, she carried on looking at Corey who waited expectantly.

'Yes,' she said finally, and they both let out a mutual sigh of relief.

'Yes, please.'

CHAPTER FOUR

STOPPING by Switchboard to pick up her pager, Lydia struggled mentally with the day ahead, wondering how she was going to play things when she saw Corey again.

His proposal of a date had floored her.

Sent her into a spin of anxiety!

Her long-awaited days off should have left her refreshed, invigorated, but instead she was completely exhausted.

For once, sleepless nights spent tossing and turning had had nothing to do with the basketball-sized bump attached to her stomach and everything to do with a certain male nurse impinging her thoughts, turning her world around with just one crook of his finger, one slow lazy smile. Suddenly the world looked different.

Suddenly she was thinking about balls and make-up again, leg waxes and deep-conditioning treatments for her increasingly wayward hair—all the things that should add up to a memorable first date but all the things a woman in her condition shouldn't even be considering.

Aside from her pregnancy, she had her job to consider. What were the staff going to think, what on earth would Dr Browne say when he found out, as he undoubtedly would? The hospital grapevine was legendary. There was probably already a notice on the staff whiteboard, outlining Corey's invitation!

You're being paranoid, Lydia scolded herself as she checked her pager and clipped it to her top pocket. The special care unit wasn't like the general wards. The intensity of the shifts didn't exactly allow for much time to observe a blossoming romance, which was probably how Gavin and Marcia's relationship had managed to go unnoticed for so long, Lydia thought grimly. For once the pressure of the unit might actually work in her favour, Lydia reasoned as she made her way along the highly polished corridor. No one was any the wiser, and Corey would be too busy with his shift to notice her blushes.

Undoubtedly the day would take care of itself.

It did, of course—in fact, she never even made it to the ward. The shrill sound of her emergency pager prompted a huge kick of alarm from the baby nestled within, and even Lydia, who should be used to it by now, still caught her breath anxiously as she reached for her pager. Picking up speed as she read the message, Lydia headed for the antenatal ward, breaking into a run as the overhead loudspeaker started to crackle into life. Clearly the situation had intensified since the first page had been sent for even though all nearby doctors had to respond to an overhead alert, the individual page that had been sent clearly meant it was Lydia's skills that were called for. She formed a mental plan of attack as she ran, only pausing for one small cleansing breath as she reached the doors of the antenatal ward, knowing a calm, unruffled appearance would be more than called for.

It was!

The highly polished floors of the corridor give way to carpet tiles as she swept in, but despite the tranquil surroundings of the antenatal ward nothing could hide the urgency of the situation unfolding as Lydia registered Sinead, the midwife, carrying a grey lifeless bundle into the treatment room.

'Good morning, Doctor! It's *very* good to see you.' The lyrical Irish tones of Sinead seemed out of place with such a sick baby, but Lydia didn't miss the note of relief in her colleague's voice as Lydia followed a step behind. Both women were used to such emergencies but the tension was palpable. These first few precious moments of the baby's life were vital, would dictate the outcome, and though Sinead was ending a long and tiring shift, though Lydia had barely digested her kick-start morning coffee, both women snapped into emergency mode, fuelled on adrenaline and compassion.

This life mattered.

'Good morning, Sinead.' Lydia's eyes never left the baby, assessing him even before he was placed on the resuscitation cot, pulling out her stethoscope as Sinead deftly but gently sucked the baby's blocked airway, the thick dark fluid that came up the tube a worrying sign. 'Thick meconium,' Sinead said grimly, moving aside to let Lydia take over, suctioning the airway deeper in an effort to clear it. The meconium was the baby's first bowel action, and the fact it had been passed *in utero* was a sign the baby had been distressed. But what was of more concern now was that unless the airway was cleared, when the baby took its first breath it would drag the thick goo deep into its fragile lungs, causing horrendous problems later. Though Sinead had moved aside, they still worked together, Lydia deftly inserting an airway down the baby's nose into his lungs and again deeply suctioning, trying to clear the baby's airway of the deadly fluid before inflating his tiny lungs as Sinead gave a brief but vital handover.

'Baby Clarke,' Sinead informed Lydia as she worked on the lifeless infant. 'Thirty weeks gestation, Mum's in with—'

'Meredith,' Lydia barked, pulling the stethoscope out of her ears. 'I met her a couple of days ago. He's bradycardic. Start cardiac massage while I get an umbilical line in.'

Sinead never missed a beat, carrying on the handover as two fingers worked the tiny chest, pumping the tiny heart and hopefully pushing the oxygen Lydia was rapidly but gently delivering to the baby's brain before irreparable damage was done. 'Meredith started having contractions at seven a.m. I'd just rung Dr Hamilton to come in when she hit the buzzer and said the baby was coming—that was the first page you'd have received. I knew the baby was going to be a small one and that we'd need you, but when I examined her and saw the mec-stained liquor I put out the second emergency call. She delivered just as you arrived—we never even made it to the delivery room.'

'Where the hell is everyone?' Lydia looked up anxiously. She'd only been in the room a couple of minutes as she'd almost been passing when her pager had gone off. More hands were needed, and as another midwife and an anaesthetist dashed in and stared attaching the baby to monitors Lydia gave a grateful nod, knowing the full team would be here shortly.

She sensed Corey before she saw him. Called for a drug and knew, just knew, it was Corey behind her, pulling up the vital medicines that would be delivered into the umbilical line Lydia had deftly inserted. 'He's picking up.' There was a triumphant note in Lydia's voice as the baby grimaced, a sigh of relief so small it was barely there escaping her lips as flaccid limbs started to flicker into life, a tiny grey fist clenching into a ball as a mottled pink colour took over from the foreboding grey.

'He's pinking up nicely.' Corey moved in beside her, checking the baby's five-minute Apgar score, a vital tool to assessing how effective the resuscitation had been and a valuable indicator to the expected outcome.

'Seven.' Corey's eyes met hers for the first time. 'Which is a good pick-up from two. Well done, ladies.'

Lydia was experienced, a doctor, a registrar, but Corey was at the top of his nursing career. The last ten years of his working life had entirely focused on children as sick as this and his words gave her a small glow of pride. It *had* been a job well done, even though there was still more to do, but for now the palpable tension that had filled the treatment room lifted a notch as they worked on.

'Do you want to start antibiotics now?' he asked, and Lydia nodded. Even though she had suctioned the airway as effectively as she could, undoubtedly respiratory infection would be setting in.

'What have we here?' Dr Browne's booming voice

filled the room and everyone stepped back slightly as he examined the infant, barely acknowledging though undoubtedly listening to Lydia's handover.

'What was his due date?' Dr Browne asked, not even looking up, gently examining the baby's head, checking for any anomalies, placing a finger into the infant's mouth and checking for deformities. Normally Lydia would have deferred to the midwife then, or rummaged through the notes to come up with a speedy answer, but this morning there was no need.

This morning the answer was on the tip of her tongue.

'January the twenty-second.'

Her voice was soft, the slight waver not even noticed by all gathered, and as naïve as it sounded for someone so qualified, perhaps for the first time it hit Lydia that inside her wasn't just a foetus, a baby, but a person, a viable person that would live and breathe and grow, a person in its own right. The thought truly terrified her.

Swallowing hard, she gazed at the infant that lay before her, her hand moving instinctively to her own stomach, lost in her own world, barely registering Dr Browne's comments, only dragging her attention back to the job in hand when a strong, comforting hand rested briefly on her shoulder and Corey spoke.

'Dr Browne seems to have everything under control. Now might be a good time to have a word with the mum. I'll be back in a moment,' he added to Sinead. 'We'll get him over to the unit A.S.A.P.'

Lydia didn't wait for Dr Browne's agreement, just let Corey lead her away, infinitely grateful for his insight.

'You knew, didn't you?' Lydia said when they were finally alone. 'Knew it would get to me when I saw the baby.'

Corey nodded. 'It kind of rams things home a bit, doesn't it?' He gave a wry smile. 'I've seen it a lot when mums come down to the unit before they deliver. When they actually see a baby due around the same time as their own it's a shock, but a baby with the exact same delivery date would be a bit of a wake-up call. Especially…'

His voice trailed off and Lydia looked up sharply. 'Especially what?'

'Especially for someone still trying to get used to the idea that they're having a baby.' A hand caught hers, pulled her just a fraction towards him as Lydia screwed her eyes closed.

'You can talk to me, Lydia,' he said, softly but she shook her head fiercely.

'I need to go and see Meredith.'

Always busy, the unit surpassed itself. Baby Clarke wasn't the only admission. A twenty-three-week-gestation baby was flown in from the country that made Meredith's baby, though very sick, look positively huge. Lydia found herself in constant demand, juggling the new admissions with her other frail charges, but not for the first time it was Patrick causing the most concern, Patrick hovering on the very brink.

Patrick breaking Corey's heart.

'How's he doing?' Lydia ventured as she stopped by Patrick's incubator, long after her shift should have ended, her bag hanging off her shoulder, her hair coiling its way out of the French roll she had attempted some fourteen hours ago.

'The same,' Corey said softly, his eyes flicking up. 'I was just giving him his antibiotics. I do have a reason to be here.'

'He's not out of bounds, Corey,' Lydia said softly. 'I just thought you were…'

'You were right.'

His admission surprised her and she gave a relieved smile, glad he was able to see the problem.

'Would you believe me if I told you I never normally do?' Corey murmured, dragging his eyes away from his patient to meet hers. 'Get involved, that is. Oh, there's been a couple here and there, a few times when I've known I had to step back, but normally it's the parents who upset me—you know the type, years of IVF and this baby's their one and only chance. Normally it's them I feel sorry for, the parents I'm fighting for.'

'Not in this case.'

Their gazes drifted back to Patrick, to a little guy hanging on by a thread with no one in his corner to fight for him, no one except an unlikely looking nurse who badly needed a shave and a doctor who needed her bed.

'I *was* comparing him to Bailey, was comparing Jenny's situation to Adele's, but that's not the only reason I got so close. The simple fact is, this little guy's special in his own right.'

She watched as he put his hand through the port-hole, brushed the downy furrowed brow with his massive hands. For an appalling moment Lydia felt the sting of tears at the back of her eyes.

'He knows my voice.'

'I'm sure he does—you speak to him enough.' Her voice was a bit too loud, a touch too harsh, but it was better than breaking down. 'Come on, you.' Lydia hitched her bag up an inch, chewed on her lip for a fraction of a second and chose to ignore the voice of reason that was begging her to reconsider. 'I'll buy you a drink.'

She didn't, of course.

Corey bought it, making sure she was seated in the pavement café outside before disappearing into the bar, leaving Lydia alone with her frenzied thoughts.

What the hell had she been thinking of?

The ball in two weeks had been enough to contend with and here she was speeding things along, asking him, *asking him*, for a drink, inviting him to get closer.

'I said I'd get them,' Lydia grumbled as he placed a long glass of iced grapefruit juice in front of her.

'You can get the next round.' Corey shrugged, taking a long sip of his beer as Lydia's brain shot into overdrive. He'd be asking for a menu next!

If ever there had been an uncomfortable silence, this was the one that would go down in history. Finally, as Lydia sucked on air and twisted her straw through ice cubes, it was Corey who finally broke the drought.

'So what do you think people would make of us?'

'Sorry?' Frowning, Lydia looked up.

'The people-watchers. What would they make of us?'

Lydia gave a small shrug. 'Two colleagues out for

a quick drink after work,' she suggested, knowing it was a poor attempt. Corey's rueful laugh only confirmed the fact.

'I think we look like one of those miserable married couples you see—you know the type.' Corey grinned, not remotely fazed by her scowl. 'The ones who sit there and don't say anything to each other, just stare at the menu and fiddle with their straws.'

Letting go of her straw, Lydia looked up and gave a wry smile.

'No,' she corrected, 'you're not doing it right, that's way too basic. Of course they'd assume the baby's yours and, given that we've both got briefcases, they'd rightly assume we'd both been at work.' Chewing on her bottom lip, she thought for a moment, missing Corey's smile as her forehead creased endearingly. 'They'd think I'm exhausted, which is right, but they'd be thinking I resent you because I still have to work and that you're feeling guilty because I am.'

'So we've got money problems?' Corey grinned as Lydia nodded.

'That's not the half of it. You're wondering what on earth happened to the sexy, skinny thing you dated last summer...'

'And you're wondering what happened to that laid-back, easygoing guy of yesteryear?'

They both laughed, the ice well and truly broken.

'So what do I do for a living?'

Corey eyed her thoughtfully. 'Lawyer, doctor, accountant...'

'Utterly predictable.'

'But charmingly so. What about me?'

'Well…' Lydia started a smile on the edge of her full lips. 'It galls me to say it, given that I'm the expert, that I pride myself on my observation skills and everything, but never in a million years would I have come up with a special care nurse.'

'What would you have come up with?' Corey asked as Lydia stared for a full minute.

'The briefcase would have thrown me, but I could have put it down to a bulging contract,' she said triumphantly. 'Rugby league, semi-retired and about to start coaching.'

'Very good!' The admiration in his voice caught Lydia by surprise. She had been half joking, but when Corey carried on talking her mouth dropped open at her own astuteness. 'It was footy actually—Australian Rules football. I was an emerging ruckman, should have been coming to the end of an illustrious career about now and, yes, I guess coaching would have held a certain appeal.'

'You were a footballer?'

'Nearly.' He drained his glass and Lydia waited for him to elaborate, but just as she thought a second round was approaching, just as she thought maybe a menu wouldn't be such a bad idea after all, Corey glanced at his watch and stood up.

'I've got to go.' The reluctance in his voice seemed genuine but still Lydia felt a stab of disappointment that the evening had to end so soon. 'I promised Bailey I'd drop in tonight…'

Lydia looked at her own watch. 'But it's after nine. Shouldn't he be in bed?'

Corey gave a dry smile. 'That's why I have to go.'

They headed to their cars, parked side by side, and

the silence that should have been easy now suddenly felt deafening. Lydia felt as awkward as a teenager on her first date as she rummaged in her bag for her keys, could feel the weight of his eyes on her as she pressed the button, jumping with nerves as the lights flashed and the car unlocked.

'Night. then,' she mumbled, not even looking up, brushing past him, desperate for the safety of her car, desperate to ignore the sexual vibes pulsing in the warm evening air around them.

''Night.' His wrist closed around hers, pulling her back gently, and because her lousy parking attempt ensured a confined space between the cars, because she was pregnant, there was no hope of standing apart. For a moment she felt her bump brush against him, felt the weight of the child that was coming between them in so many more ways than one, and for a guilty moment Lydia wished it wasn't so.

Wished they were just another couple, starting out, sharing a drink, a kiss perhaps, with no more on their minds than the heady rush of a fledgling romance.

He traced a finger along her cheek and, despite the warm night air, Lydia shivered with expectancy at his mere touch. She was struggling to breathe now, terribly so, her body burning with awareness. There was a final moment of clarity as his face moved towards hers, a final grasp at reason, the inner voice to remind her it couldn't possibly work. Then his lips were on hers, the blistering effect of him close, so close, blowing reason into the hazy horizon as she revelled in the joy of exploring him, the taste, that heady masculine smell, the bliss of being held in such strong arms, shoulders so wide her arms barely met the sides.

Yes, it was only a kiss, but it held so much promise, such a teasing, tempting glimpse of the man she was starting to adore, it took all her strength to finally pull her lips away.

'You have to go,' she whispered, reluctance in every word.

'I know.' Corey said equally reluctantly. 'But you know I'd give anything to stay?' His arms were still wrapped around her, the swell of her stomach pressing into him, and Lydia nodded, because she did know, she knew exactly how he felt.

This was only the start.

CHAPTER FIVE

EYEING herself in the mirror, for the first time in recent memory Lydia felt a shiver of excitement ripple through her.

She felt sexy.

Oh, not drop-dead gorgeous or anything like that, but the heavy purple dress seemed made for her. OK, maybe it showed way too much creamy bosom but at least it detracted from her stomach and the splits down the sides were seductive rather than tarty, showing just enough sheer stockinged leg encased in jewelled high-heeled sandals which had truly been her only splurge for the event.

Apart from the handbag.

Apart from the foundation that swore it would give her a dewy glow.

And mascara wasn't a luxury item, Lydia consoled herself—it was an essential.

Not for a second when she had taken in her rather unflattering black maternity dress to the dry cleaner's had she expected the assistant to tell her about unclaimed dresses for sale.

Barely able to contain her excitement, she had purchased, for hardly more than the price of cleaning her old faithful, a gorgeous deep purple beaded dress. And now as she stood in front of the mirror, adding just one more curl with her hair wand, Lydia actually felt pleased with her appearance, excited at the prospect of a night with Corey, a night away from the hospital, a night away from her lonely, rather large house, ready for a night with a man who was undoubtedly special.

But how could it possibly work?

The question was a mocking taunt that had been plaguing her for days now. From tentative kisses passion had grown, and Lydia knew, just knew that tonight things would be going further, wanted them to, come to that. But what then?

Sinking onto the side of the bed, Lydia buried her face in her trembling hands, willing the impossible conundrums to end, trying to push away the image of child-care centres, nappies, bottles and the endless guilt that would surely come with it. She had already taken on way, way too much. She should be focusing on her baby, her career, not buying new sheets, not changing the bed in case…

Staring at her bedside phone, she took a deep breath. She should ring Corey, tell him she'd made a mistake, plead a migraine, plead temporary insanity if that was what it would take to end what should never have been started.

As if on cue, the doorbell rang and the nerves that had finally caught up seemed to choke her. She would tell him face to face, call a halt now. Taking the stairs slowly in unfamiliar high heels, she saw his outline through the stained glass panel, the breadth of his shoulders, saw his shadow smooth his hair and fiddle with his shirt collar.

Pulling the front door open, she smiled shyly as Corey eyed her a moment. 'You look stunning,' he said slowly, and from the admiration in his eyes Lydia knew that he meant it.

'Not quite black velvet,' Lydia said, and she chewed nervously on her bottom lip. 'Corey, about tonight...' she started, her voice trailing off as he gave her a slow smile.

'Having second thoughts?'

A small nod followed a nervous swallow. She could feel the sweat on her palms as she gripped the doorhandle, utterly unable to meet his eyes. 'I don't know what I was thinking. I should never have agreed to come.'

'Why did you, then?'

She hesitated for a moment before answering. 'I wanted to,' Lydia admitted, dragging her eyes up to his, 'but I just don't see how—'

'Would it help if I told you I'm nervous, too?' Corey broke in. 'Would it help if I told you that I've been asking myself the same sort of questions?' When she didn't answer he carried on gently. 'Lydia, the easiest thing in the world would be to say that this isn't a date, that this is just a work do, two colleagues sharing an evening. I've even tried that line on myself, but I know it's not true. This is big and it's scary and if we actually sat down and thought about it we'd probably both run a mile. I nearly rang and cancelled.'

Even though she'd been about to do the same thing, his admission startled her. 'Then why didn't you?'

He paused for an age. 'Because I wanted to see you and in the end it overrode my doubts. Lydia, I don't know where this is going to lead and I don't know how we're going to deal with all the questions

that being together will throw up. All I know is how
I feel about you and for now that's enough for me.
But is it for you?'

She let his words sink in, pondered on his question
for a moment, curiously pleased that he had doubts,
that he was taking it as seriously as her, until finally
she nodded, her face breaking into her first genuine
smile since he'd arrived. 'Do you want to come in for
a moment?'

'I'd love to, but we'd better get going. I promised
we'd be there early.'

His refusal left her strangely disappointed. She'd
been cleaning for days now, well, not cleaning exactly, she'd thrown some bleach in the loo and moved
a rather large ironing basket to the safer confines of
a cupboard and bought some fancy coffee-beans, even
put some fresh flowers in the lounge and bought a
few beers in case he wanted one, which theoretically
could be considered another splurge!

Taking a wrap from over the banister, Lydia
wrapped it around her then collected her bag, locking
and checking the door behind her, pushing doubts
aside, determined to have a good evening, to get to
know the man beside her that bit better. She finally
took his arm and headed off to his rather nice, rather
luxury-looking car.

'They pay nurses too much.' Lydia grinned, lowering herself into the leather passenger seat.

'Don't tell anyone.'

Craning her head, she took in the child safety seat
in the back, out of place in this rather male car.

'For Bailey?'

Corey nodded.

'How is he?'

'For once he's not hyped up on red cordial and fast food. He's at my parents' this week.' He took his eyes off the road for a second and gave Lydia a brief eye roll. 'Adele's gone away to Queensland for a week with some new "friends" she's made.'

Lydia heard the quotation marks around the word and frowned. 'It doesn't sound as if you approve.'

'I don't,' Corey said tightly. 'She's hanging around with a group of, I don't know what you'd call them. They're off at some festival on the coast and no doubt Adele's the one financing the booze. She got a lot of compensation from the accident and seems to be doing her level best to blow it. She wants to have fun, figures she deserves it, and though I know it's not Adele's fault as such, know that I shouldn't get cross...'

'You do.'

Corey shook his head. 'Never at her, but inside...' he let out a low ragged sigh and Lydia's heart went out to him.

'Maybe you need to, Corey,' she suggested tentatively. 'What's happened might not have been Adele's fault, but if she's going to be Bailey's mother she needs to take some sort of responsibility for him.'

'You were right when you suggested I was comparing Adele to Jenny.' He glanced over and Lydia gave a rueful nod. She took no pleasure in being right. 'But the most ironic part of it is that Adele was the most responsible woman I've ever met. The old Adele would be appalled at the way Bailey was being bought up. Hell, Adele was even a responsible child. She used to recycle things long before it became fashionable, spent her pocket money on an alarm clock when she was six years old so she'd never be late for school. You should have seen her when Bailey was a baby.'

'She was a good mother?' Lydia asked, and noticed the pain behind his slow nod.

'She was, but I'm starting to realise that Adele's gone now and no amount of wishing is going to bring her back.' She could see his knuckles clenched around the steering-wheel, see the tension in his shoulders, and her heart went out to him. Lydia had seen it before, worked on a neuro ward during her internship and seen the devastation of brain injury, the torture families faced when their loved one returned a different person. 'My parents have tried to persuade her to move in with them, I've even offered for the two of them to live with me. Not that my flat's particularly suitable, but at least that way I could be sure Bailey was clean and fed...'

'She refused?' Lydia asked, knowing the answer before he finished, and Corey gave a weary nod.

'She's an adult. Inside that irresponsible head of hers still lurks a lawyer and Adele knows her rights, knows that we can't force her to live with us, can't force her to do anything.'

'It must be hard,' Lydia ventured, knowing her words were woefully inadequate.

'It is,' Corey agreed, then, like a light switching on, the pensive mood was gone, his face lighting up with a beautiful smile as they pulled up outside a luxury hotel. He pulled on the handbrake and turned to face her. 'Enough about our worries, huh? Let's just enjoy tonight?'

Lydia didn't need to be asked twice, and when they stepped into the ballroom, one hand of Corey's protectively around what used to be her waist, it was easy to cast problems aside, easy to smile back at the curious stares that followed them, to enjoy the delectable food and later, much later to enjoy every dance with a man who made her feel every bit a woman.

'We'll be the talk of the unit,' Lydia said, drunk on mineral water and the heady lust of a new relationship.

'We are already,' Corey said into her hair. 'And guess what? I don't care.'

'Are you sure?' Pulling back, Lydia's eyes searched his face. 'I know this isn't exactly…'

A finger pressed against her lips as he gently shushed her. 'No one plans these things, Lydia, they just happen.' His eyes never left her face, his body solid and firm against hers, and she felt ripples of lust cascade through her as he melted her with his words. 'And it's happened to us.'

It was the best night of her life.

The best.

It was as if the gods had decided she'd had enough bad luck for a while, shed enough tears, eaten enough humble pie. Even the raffle seemed preordained as Lydia's number came up and she clipped along the dance floor to claim her prize.

And because it was a special care unit ball, because most of the sponsors were baby related, it wasn't hard to see why a gorgeous white bassinet filled with every last baby essential and a few non-essentials, too, would be the pride of the table and the best prize of all!

'I never win anything.' Lydia giggled as Corey attempted to load it into his boot at the end of the evening, eventually flattening the back seat just to somehow slot it in. 'You rigged it, didn't you?'

'Shush.' Corey laughed. 'That sort of talk will get me shot and, no, for your information, I didn't rig it. I guess this must just be your lucky night.'

It *was* her lucky night, Lydia decided with relish.

She felt lucky! Lucky and alive, even funny and beautiful too.

Of course, she couldn't possibly lift the bassinet out of the car, so naturally Corey had to, and once he was inside her home it seemed silly not to offer him a coffee. As she nervously opened the front door, watching as he dwarfed her hallway with his presence, it felt so nice to be coming home with someone, not just anyone but that special someone.

'Three sugars, isn't it?' Her voice was high and slightly breathless as she went into the kitchen, fiddled with cups, looked everywhere but at him as she prepared the brew. Achingly aware, she held her breath as he came up behind her, her hands trembling over the cups, his eyes burning holes in her shoulders as she struggled to concentrate on this most basic task and try to make some small talk.

The espresso cups were side by side, the sound of the grinder filling the tense silence, and because she had no idea what to do, she didn't move, didn't turn around; just watched as the black brew trickled into the cups. As the grinder whirred into action, preparing the beans for the next cup, Lydia couldn't help wondering whether Corey would be there to share it.

For a futile moment she pretended not to notice his hand toying with a tendril of hair at the nape of her neck, pretended not to notice hot lips locating the place where her neck met her shoulder, and tried to focus on a world that was curiously blurry as fingers stroked the length of her bare arms, as those lips blazed a steady trail up the hollows of her neck.

How she wanted to turn around.

How she wanted to kiss him.

To get it over with sort of thing.

To get this awkward, tentative moment out of the way, to somehow fast forward this bit and head straight for the bedroom, to find out once and for all if the sexual chemistry was as real as she had imagined.

He turned her round to face him, the answer right there in his eyes, but just as their lips met, just as the tentative kisses they had shared to date became deeper, more urgent, another rather important question decided to rear its head, or foot, or elbow, Lydia wasn't sure which, as the baby decided to make its presence felt.

'It's got no sense of occasion,' Lydia said as Corey jumped slightly, the surprise in his face evident, an incredulous grin parting his wide sensual mouth. But as his hand moved down to her stomach, cupping her bump, cradling the swollen, ripe mound as she gazed downwards, as beautiful as the image was, it threw up more questions than it answered, questions that needed to faced if they were to move on.

'It's not yours, Corey.' If her words sounded harsh,

she didn't mean them to. If it was too severe or too blatant, she didn't care. This was too important to skirt around the edges.

'I know.' Still his hand remained, but his eyes lifted to Lydia's. 'And if you'd asked me to describe my ideal woman a few weeks ago, seven months pregnant with another man's baby wouldn't have sprung to mind.'

His honesty didn't faze her. She was glad, so glad they could go there, tiny wings of hope fluttering inside as they faced their issues head-on.

'And now?'

'I'm crazy about you, Lydia.' The honesty in his voice moved her. 'And I know it's not the ideal, I know we've got a lot to face, but I really believe we can do it. I really believe that if we want to, we can make this work.'

'It just seems to have happened so quickly. It just seems such a strange time to be…' She couldn't say it, couldn't quite reveal the depth of her feelings, but Corey had no such reserve.

'To be falling in love?' he finished for her, and Lydia nodded.

'Maybe we should wait till after the baby's here,' Lydia suggested, appalled at the very thought but truly confused. Never had it entered her head that she might feel like this at this late stage in her pregnancy. After Gavin, after the anger and hurt of the past, love had seemed but a distant dream, a dream she hadn't had time to even contemplate, such had been the struggle to merely keep her head above the swirling water of her misery. Yet here it was, knocking at her door, asking not only to be let in but possibly to stay.

'Perhaps it would be wiser to wait, to put things on hold for a while and see how we feel once it's here.'

'It!' Corey's grin made her smile. 'You really need to come up with a pet name for that bump of yours.' His voice grew more serious. 'I don't want to rush you, Lydia, don't want you to do anything you're not sure of, but I don't think waiting till after the baby's here is a good idea. If that's what you really want then I'll try and put my feelings on hold for a while, but I really think we need some time while it is just the two of us, some time to get our heads around the idea of being a couple, some time to work all the big things out.' His words made sense. 'This is the most important time of your life and if we're going to have any sort of future together then surely it's better that I'm there for you.'

He watched as his words sank in, watched as she rolled them through her mind, those deep eyes searching his as she contemplated all he was offering. 'There's just one thing I need to know, Lydia...'

'Then ask,' Lydia said softly. 'Now's surely the time.'

'What if Gavin changes his mind, what if when the baby comes...?'

'It's over,' she whispered.

'For you perhaps, but...'

It was Lydia taking the lead now, Lydia silencing him with a finger to his lips. 'I can't speak for Gavin, but I know how I feel, Corey, and I don't want him in my life. The day I found out he'd brought a third person into our marriage it was irrefutably over for me and Gavin knew that, knew that infidelity, for

whatever reason, was the one thing I simply would
never forgive.'

'I believe you,' Corey said softly, clearly moved
by her answer, but she sensed the hesitation in his
voice. 'What if he wants to see the baby, Lydia? What
if once the baby's here, he wants some part in its
life?'

'I can't see that happening,' Lydia answered honestly. 'And that hurts me. Not for me, I hope you can
believe that, but for the baby. As much as my feelings
are over for Gavin, I hope for the baby's sake that
there will be some sort of relationship between them,
though in my heart I don't think it's possible. Gavin's
too busy with his new life, too wrapped up in his new
girlfriend to want a reminder of the past. But if he
does want to see the baby, I'm not going to deny him,
but that's for the baby's sake, not mine.'

'You really are over him.' It was more a statement
than a question but Lydia nodded firmly. Never had
she been more sure of anything in her life. And not
just about her feelings for Gavin. Standing before her
was a man who made her feel more like a woman
than she had ever felt, who thrilled her, excited her,
made her weak just thinking about him. A man who
could make her day with a smile or end it with a
scowl and though maybe they should have been, the
asks weren't quite so tough any more, everything was
crystal clear.

'The coffee's getting cold,' Lydia whispered, even
though coffee was the last thing on her mind.

'I don't want coffee,' Corey admitted. 'I never did.'

Which left them with two choices. And as she
slipped out of his embrace and walked down the hall-

way, seeing his crestfallen expression as she reached the front door, Lydia was scarcely able to suppress her smile.

'Can I ring you?' Corey asked, fiddling with his keys in his pocket and clearly perturbed at the sudden change in her. 'We could talk again tomorrow, before we go back to work…'

'I'm tired of talking, so tired, in fact, that I'm going to bed.' A cheeky smile played on her lips as she climbed the steps. 'Oh, and, Corey, would you mind bringing up the bassinet?' Turning, she leant over the banister as his expression snapped to stunned. 'And turn out the hall light on your way up, would you?'

CHAPTER SIX

THE feeling of empowerment left Lydia at the top of the stairs.

The enormity of what was transpiring hit its mark as she heard Corey's footsteps on the stairs. She stood trembling in the shadows, listening as he approached.

What the hell was she doing?

The words were a mocking taunt as he reached the top of the stairs, a vast moon drifting past her hall window illuminating his beauty, capturing the sheer magnificence of the man who slowly walked towards her.

She was pregnant, for heaven's sake. Oh, she'd read her magazines, even flicked through the articles that insisted she was at her most sensual, pumping hormones, the epitome of femininity. But somehow it didn't sit quite right, somehow she didn't feel brave or gorgeous, didn't quite feel up to the scrutiny she had so recently invited.

'I forgot the crib!'

His admission, the whole supposed reason for him coming up, obviously forgotten in his sheer haste to get to her, caused a ripple of nervous laughter to escape her lips, but it came out too loud, too false and Corey noticed.

'We don't have to do this.' His hand captured her wrist, his fingers closing around it, her radial pulse flicking a nervous tune as he held her at arm's length, his eyes searching her face. 'We don't have to do anything unless you're sure.'

'I don't know if I'm ready.' The darkness helped, made it easier to admit the truth, and softened the blush that surely scorched her face. 'I just never anticipated something like this happening while I was pregnant, never imagined feeling like this so soon after...' Her voice trailed off, her ex-husband's name holding no part in this precious moment. 'I don't know anything, Corey, except that I don't want you to go.'

'Then I won't,' Corey said simply.

'I'm just not sure if I'm ready to...'

'Then we won't,' Corey said just as simply, but loaded with caring. He led her to the bedroom as surely as if it were his, and Lydia stood frozen with expectation and trepidation as he undressed her slowly, undid the straps of her heels, sliding the zip down on her dress as her trembling hands pulled up the curls that had strayed. He even took out her earrings, pulling out the little butterflies and laying the shimmering crystals side by side on her dressing-table before taking her by the hand and leading her to the bed. He laid her down, the cool cotton of the sheet floating over her as she lay, eyes half-closed, shyly watching as he undressed, her body tingling with anticipation as he climbed in beside her and pulled her close. Not a single word was uttered, just a world of affection in each and every touch.

And while it was lovely and everything, while it was wonderful to be held, wonderful to be wrapped in his embrace, for not a single demand to be made and all that, somewhere along the way, and Lydia was never sure exactly at which point, but somewhere between the delicious homecoming of his skin on hers, somewhere between the lazy, decadent bliss of the twilight zone they had created, simple affection wasn't enough. Those arms wrapped around her needed to be tighter, the scratch of his thighs pressed into the curve of hers wasn't quite deep enough and she wriggled slightly, one breast shifting a delicious centimetre, the soft underside nuzzling his palm. As she felt his breathing quicken so too did hers. She could feel her inhibitions drifting away, probably joining her earrings somewhere on the other side of the room as she nuzzled her body into his, moved another tiny centimetre till her nipple lay a hair's breath from his fingers. His low groan was an entirely unnecessary confirmation of his longing as she felt the swell of his arousal nudging the back of her thigh, and she felt as beautiful, as wanted and as sexy as she'd ever felt in her life! Turning to face him, she stared into the dark pools of his eyes before closing hers in bliss as his lips met hers, the chemistry that had always been there, patiently waiting in the wings, an attraction that had permeated since their first meeting affirmed now, ready to explode in heated unison as his tongue probed her mouth, as their passion deepened.

And it felt marvellous to be held, skin on skin, hands exploring, the sheet impatiently kicked off, and though the light was off a thoughtful full moon allowed for visual exploration, allowed Lydia to marvel at the man who lay beside.

Of course, one should never compare, naturally it was rude, but for a tiny stolen moment Lydia thought she had died and gone to heaven, scarcely able to believe she had sole access to the man that lay beside her.

Man!

Every part of him, every delicious inch of him screamed masculinity. Just lying beside him, he dwarfed her with the sheer size of him. From the mat of dark hair on his wide chest to the flat, toned stomach, he was perfect. Trembling, she ran her fingers gently down the decadent line of hair and took him in her hand, so wide and swollen, so alive in her hand, that for a moment Lydia felt a well of panic. Sure, she'd read the books, she was a doctor, for heaven's sake, but so magnificent was the parcel of masculinity she held in her palms, surely it was going to hurt.

He misinterpreted her trepidation and she adored him for it, adored the fact her feelings came first.

'We don't have to do this.'

His was the voice of reason, for Lydia was past the point of no return.

'Oh, but we do,' she moaned as his fingers snaked inside her. Almost weeping with anticipation, a tiny shudder building inside her as the palm of his hand grazed the swollen nub of her womanhood, the marshmallows of her thighs parting as she arched her body closer, a silent plea for him to enter, such was the need to have him inside her overriding everything else.

He was gentle, so gentle, the soft swell of her stomach ensuring he entered her slowly, but even so she gasped as he filled her, digging her nails into his back, her eyes screwing closed at the sheer presence of him, clinging to his back as he started to move, almost bracing herself to accommodate him. But suddenly her body was moving of its own accord, dragging him deeper, one leg coiling around his buttocks as the shudder that had hummed in the distance proliferated with alarming speed, her orgasm creeping up on her with determined stealth, catching her utterly unprepared and unexpected. She felt as if she were having some sort of amazing out-of-body experience, watching from above their bodies inextricably entwined, moving, moving, coiling, riding together, absolutely in rhythm, completely in sync, a sensual dance that had seemingly been rehearsed for weeks. She could almost see the white pearl of her neck as she threw her head back, her face contorting in frenzied concentration as her body moved of its own accord, a shuddering orgasm, so deep, so violent it literally took her breath away. She could almost see the tension in his shoulders as she clung on for dear life, Corey swelling within her, more if that were possible, then ragged, gasping breaths, an almost guttural groan as he buried his face in her neck, the glisten of sweat creating a steaming sheen as they slid together, their bodies slowly relaxing, the thrum of their hearts pounding in unison, their low, breathless gasps as the world slowly came back. And still there was nothing said, for nothing needed to be said, just a murmured goodnight as he softly repositioned her then pulled her back into his arms, the infinitely safe feeling only his embrace allowed. His hand strong and warm on her stomach as she drifted off to sleep.

Corey stayed awake, listening to her breathing, the tickle of her hair on his cheek, which should have

annoyed but curiously didn't, the thud of her baby
swooping against his hand, occasionally nudging his
palm. He wondered how she could sleep, how each
and every movement didn't waken her, smiling into
the darkness as the baby warmed to its audience, her
whole stomach alive beneath his hand awakening
feelings he had never anticipated, curiously protective
instincts, not just for the woman he held but for the
baby within her.

Feelings that felt suspiciously like love.

CHAPTER SEVEN

LYDIA awoke to the delicious aroma of coffee and hot buttered toast, but better still—a tender kiss.

'How long have you been up?' Lydia yawned, stretching like a cat and then giggling as Corey captured one ankle that had escaped from under the rumpled sheet.

'For a couple of hours.' His hand moved to her stomach. 'I had a rather rude awakening. I think it might have been a foot in my rib—how on earth do you sleep with all that going on?'

'It's like a leaking tap,' Lydia said. 'You learn to live with it.'

Blinking, Lydia focused on her alarm clock, her eyes widening as she realised it was after ten. 'I never oversleep,' she gasped, but Corey just smiled.

'You must have a clear conscience.'

'I do.'

She was speaking the truth. From the second she'd awoken she'd half expected a thud of guilt or shame to knock on the door, for the happiness she had found to crumble as reality had crept in, but nothing, nothing had marred the joy she had felt on awakening, not a tinge of regret clouded last night.

'I have to go.' She could hear the apologetic note in his voice as he gazed down at her. 'I don't want to,' he added immediately when Lydia opened her mouth to speak. 'It's just with Adele being in

Queensland, well, Bailey's a lot of work and he's just too much for my parents to deal with without some sort of break. I said I'd take him out for the day to give them a bit of a rest.'

He ran a reluctant hand along her cheek, before standing and pulling the trousers of his dinner suit on. Lydia lay back, her dark curls cascading on the pillows, watching as he pulled on a white shirt as crumpled as the sheet that almost covered her, rolling up the sleeves and doing up the buttons halfway before attempting to locate his cufflinks.

'I'd better go home and change first.'

'You'd better,' Lydia replied, 'and if I ever find your cufflinks I'll send them on.'

It was a joke, but for the first time he missed her humour. 'I'm not running out, Lydia. If I hadn't already promised my parents—'

'I was joking.'

He gave a small smile, picked up his rather hastily discarded cufflinks from the carpet and pocketed them. Never had a man looked more desirable, standing in the rumpled remains of a dinner suit, stubble dusting his chin and utter adoration in his eyes.

'Did it never occur to you to ask me to come?'

'You're telling me now that you faked it?' The humour was back and Lydia welcomed it, even though it was short-lived, his eyes growing serious suddenly as he lowered himself onto the edge of the bed and gave a small tight smile before capturing her hand. 'It did occur to me,' Corey said slowly. 'In fact, it's all I've thought about since I woke up. But, Lydia, this isn't going to be a romantic day out, this isn't going to be the two of us walking hand in hand on a beach and getting to know each other more. Bailey's hard work. I love him, adore him, but not by any stretch of the imagination could I say I relish the thought of a day at the beach with him.'

'Corey...' With her free hand she captured his chin, turned her to face him. 'If we're serious about getting to know each other, wouldn't this be the ideal opportunity? I admit, I'm not quite ready to meet your parents yet, but surely you could take me with you. Bailey's a huge part of your life which means, if we're going to carry this on, he's going to be a huge part of my life, too.'

His hand that had been holding hers moved, tracing her collar bone before moving down over her baby in an almost instinctive gesture, smiling at the rumblings that were still going on, regardless of the occasion.

'Anyway,' Lydia smiled, her hand over his, welling for a moment on the child within, 'who's to say this one will be an angel?'

Corey let out a low laugh. 'Oh, it will be—compared to Bailey.'

'He's four years old,' Lydia said. 'How difficult can he be?

Famous last words!

Self-conscious in short denim shorts and a white cheesecloth-type number that showed rather too much cleavage to really qualify as a maternity top, Lydia climbed into the passenger seat as Corey loaded the boot with her vague attempt at a picnic.

'Hi, Bailey,' Lydia ventured as Bailey's eyes fleetingly glanced over then effectively dismissed her, returning his attention instead to kicking back of the driver's seat with two chubby legs. 'I'm Lydia. We met once before!' Mentally kicking herself at her rather formal introduction, Lydia tried a different tack, utterly unsure how one spoke to a four-year-old. 'Are you looking forward to going to the beach?' Lydia asked helplessly, grateful when Corey climbed in and took over the rather one-sided conversation.

'We're not moving till you stop kicking, Bailey.' He flashed a smile at Lydia who stared out of windscreen and they waited, waited for the incessant kicking to stop.

'I've got all day, Bailey,' Corey warned, this time with effect. 'Good boy.' Turning, he smiled at the little boy. 'This is Lydia, she's a friend of mine and she's coming with us today. I've been telling her what a star you've been this week for Nanny and Granddad.' The tiny wink was for Lydia's benefit only as he carried on talking to his nephew. 'So let's all go and have some fun.'

Corey got about as much response as Lydia and the drive to the beach was rather uncomfortable, Corey attempting conversation and Lydia painfully aware of mistrusting eyes checking out the back of her head.

St Kilda on a balmy Sunday afternoon was breathtaking, though there was nothing sedate about the scenery. The foreshore pumped with vibrant energy, skateboarders webbing and weaving along the track, dodging power walkers and cyclists, the craft market in full swing as young and old walked hand in hand. The sparkling bay laced with jetskis, boats, serious swimmers and splashing toddlers, the excited screams from the roller-coaster at Luna Park, occasionally drowned by blasts of music from various speakers as they walked along.

Bailey reminded Lydia of a naughty puppy straining at the leash. Corey kept his hand firmly clamped around his nephew's wrist, but it proved little deterrent, Bailey somehow managing to knock over a thankfully cheap but none the less gorgeous hand-painted money box from one of the stalls, which Corey instantly coughed up for. They moved to the walking track and Corey hoisted him firmly on his shoulders.

'I can carry the basket,' Lydia said. 'I'm not completely useless.'

'I'm fine,' Corey said easily. 'Anyway, we'll stop soon. The beach is a bit clearer further up. We can have something to eat and hopefully Bailey can burn off a bit of energy.'

Which was a good idea and everything, but Lydia's version of a picnic differed somewhat from Bailey's, and she watched with mounting tension as he systematically fed the contents of his paper plate to a rapidly growing flock of seagulls.

'I don't think chicken and avocado rolls are quite his thing.' Corey grinned, seemingly unfazed as the apple juice Lydia poured was promptly spat out and thrown into the dry sand. 'Have you got any crisps?'

'I thought you said you were trying to wean him off junk food,' Lydia flustered, producing some rice crackers then putting them back in the basket as Bailey scowled at her offerings.

'I'm trying to buy us five minutes' peace,' Corey responded, as relaxed as ever, but seeing the tension in her face he stood up and produced a beach ball from the back of his backpack which he blew up in two easy breaths. 'Come on, Bailey,' he called, shooting her a wink, 'we may be gone some time.'

He wasn't exaggerating! Surely this would exhaust Bailey, surely an hour running on the beach, kicking a ball, would have some effect. Watching for a while, Lydia finally gave in and lay back on the rug as the hot sun and the sound of lapping waves finally worked their magic, watching through half-closed eyes as Corey, dressed only in shorts, managed to rival David Beckham in the divine stakes, his bronzed body gleaming, muscles outlined, all having the strangest effect on Lydia.

The strangest!

To date sex had been sex, sometimes nice, sometimes necessary, sometimes downright inconvenient, certainly not comparable with the tingling, heightened awareness Corey created just by his presence! Last night had been a revelation. Corey had awoken in her feelings she hadn't even known existed, emotions that had never been tapped. But it wasn't just the sex, Lydia mused as she lay there watching him. The heady cocktail of brute strength and compassion, the way he made her feel, the way he made her laugh— it was the whole damn package she wanted.

Or most of it.

She wasn't proud of the way she was feeling, wasn't proud of the knot of tension that tightened as her gaze drifted to Bailey. Corey had spelt it out, had told her that despite the basket today wasn't going to be a picnic as such, but she had dismissed his warnings, desperate to be let in, to glimpse every part of him.

And Bailey was a part of him, more, so much more than a nephew. He was a child that clearly had special needs and it would seem from what Corey had told her that he was the one fulfilling them.

'Hey, sleepyhead.' Corey was standing over her, his curls whipped by the salty wind, eyes crinkling against the low afternoon sun as he smiled down at her. Never had he looked more desirable. 'I don't want to jinx us, but I think I've finally worn him out!' Nodding, he gestured over to Bailey who was kneeling down, patting the sand into some sort of shape, playing quietly like a normal four-year-old.

Propping herself up on her elbow, Lydia wriggled slightly, giving him a couple more inches of the blanket as he lowered himself beside her.

'How are you doing?'

Lydia gave a small lazy shrug. 'Feeling guilty about dozing off.'

'Don't be daft. You must be exhausted. How many weeks are you now?'

'Thirty-two and counting.'

'Well into the fortnightly visits, then!'

She smiled at his acumen. What other guy on earth would understand the importance of finally hitting the fortnightly visit mark? For ever she'd sat in Dr Hamilton's waiting room, relatively slim, scarcely able to believe she'd ever hit the ranks of the final trimester, scarcely able to believe that one day she'd be massaging her own bump and talking about due dates and swabs, pethidine or agony.

'I've got an ultrasound tomorrow.' She saw concern flicker in his eyes and quickly put his mind at rest. 'It's nothing serious, it's more for my peace of mind than anything. I know it seems hard to believe, given my beached whale status, but apparently I was a tiny bit on the small side last visit. Dr Hamilton was happy to wait and see but I pushed for a scan.'

'Fair enough,' Corey mused. 'If all it does is put your mind at rest then it will worth it. I'd be the same.' He grinned at her rather startled expression. 'You know what they say—a little bit of knowledge is dangerous. Are you scared?'

His question was as tagged on as it was unexpected, and it caught Lydia by surprise.

'I guess,' she admitted after a moment's thought. 'I'm just trying not to think about it. As naïve as it sounds, I still can't quite get my head around the fact I'm going to be a mother.'

'Are you starting to come around to it yet?' Corey was on lying on his stomach now, leaning up on his elbows as he idly filtered sand through long brown fingers, but his casual stance didn't mask the weight of his question.

'Come around to what?' Lydia flustered, but when finally she looked at him, the absence of scorn made her admission a touch easier. 'Not really. Does that make me awful?'

'It makes you honest,' Corey said gently. 'And you're not the only woman to feel this way, Lydia. I know you had this baby for Gavin, know you did it to save your marriage, but was there a part of you that wanted one?'

'No,' she said softly, but it was loaded with pain because she knew it wasn't the answer most people wanted to hear. 'I wanted my marriage to work—that was why I did it. I was hoping when the baby came along I'd feel differently.'

'You will,' Corey said assuredly, hearing the tremor of uncertainty in her voice.

'I just never envisaged he'd walk away.' Her eyes were glistening with tears and Corey watched as she screwed them tightly closed. 'Never dreamt that I'd be facing this on my own.'

'You're not on your own,' Corey said softly, his hand moving from the sand and taking hers, gripping it tightly until finally Lydia gripped it back.

'I can't ask you to be there—' she started, but Corey broke in.

'You didn't ask,' he said gently. 'I offered.'

'We barely know each other, Corey,' Lydia pointed out. 'Sure, we have feelings for each other—'

'They're a bit more than just feelings,' Corey broke in, but Lydia shook her head, pulling her hand away.

'In another place, another time, this would be perfect, Corey. But the fact of the matter is, in a few short weeks I'm going to be a mother, so it's way too soon to be making promises we don't know we'll be able to keep,' Lydia insisted, sure he didn't understand the magnitude of what he was getting into, bracing herself for platitudes, for empty speeches about love conquering all.

'Let's not make promises, then.' His words startled her, wary eyes finally meeting his, and this time when he held her hand she left it there. 'Let's just take things one day at a time and if there's a space there for me tomorrow, I'd really like to be there.'

'For the ultrasound?' She gulped as he nodded slowly.

'If that's OK with you.'

'Hungry!' Bailey stood over them, breaking the moment, but such was her joy at Corey's offer, Lydia even managed to laugh as Corey scolded him. 'Then you should have eaten some of the sandwiches Lydia made. There's still a couple left!'

That was enough incentive to have Bailey scampering back to his sandcastle and Lydia watched as he concentrated on the task in hand.

'I'm sorry I snapped before,' she ventured. 'I was more cross at myself than Bailey. What four-year-old wants to munch on wholemeal rolls with avocado and chicken? I should have packed something more suitable.'

'He was rude.' Corey shrugged. 'And, yes, most four-year-olds are, but Bailey takes it to the extreme. This will probably sound as if I'm making excuses for him, that I'm burying my head in the sand, but I really don't think Bailey's problems are all that serious.'

Lydia was tempted to add a comment here, but held it in check as Corey carried on.

'He was the most beautiful baby, the gentlest, most placid little guy you could meet, and maybe there's a bit of a biased uncle talking but, honestly, Lydia, you should have seen him.'

'He's changed since the accident, then?'

Surprisingly Corey shook his head. 'When he came to, he was disorientated, upset, just as you'd expect. He'd lost his dad after all and his mum was in a coma. But it was still Bailey, still the same smile, the same laugh. I just *know* the accident didn't damage him, the changes came later.' Turning, he saw the flicker of doubt in her eyes. 'Lydia, he was so loved, so very loved. Adele would have done anything for him. I even accused her of mollycoddling him once.' He grinned at the memory but it was loaded with sadness. 'I told her if she didn't watch out he was going to end up as a nerdy, awkward kid who was too scared of getting his clothes torn or his hands dirty to actually have fun.'

Lydia nearly broke in then, nearly tossed in a comment, a general observation, but as Corey carried on talking the words stuck in her throat as she stared at Bailey's little fat hands patting a sandcastle into what could never be described as a shape.

'He was sent home three times from kinder last term with nits. And before you say all kids get nits, that cleanliness has nothing to do with it, I'm going to beg to differ. Yes, kids get nits, but most mums tear off the bed linen, give them a treatment, check their kids' hair every day. They don't *forget* to check them before they send them back. Most mums cut their kids' nails, make sure that their clothes are clean.' There was a wobble in his voice that was so alien to his usual demeanour that Lydia put her hand out, resting it on his thigh as he carried on talking. As delicious as his thigh was, it didn't even register, such was her need to comfort him as he told his story. 'He smelt, Lydia.' She watched as his jaw tightened. 'My nephew was the smelly kid, the one the others picked on, but instead of going home to a bath and bedroom stories he had to deal with Mum's new boyfriend or being dragged down to the bottle shop.'

'He's beautiful,' Lydia whispered, but Corey shook his head.

'Because I bath him every day, I cut his nails and take him to the barber's, I put out clean clothes. And the saddest part of it all is that he's four bloody years old and he dresses himself, gets up in the morning and knows that if he puts on the clothes Uncle Corey put out, maybe, just maybe he won't be teased today.'

'Oh, Corey, I'm sorry.' It was Lydia with a tremble to her voice now, Lydia staring at Bailey and trying not to cry. He must have felt them looking because suddenly Bailey stood up, kicking at the sandcastle for an impatient moment before running back to where they sat.

'Hungry!' he demanded again.

'Why don't we get something to eat?' Lydia suggested, nodding to the hotel that glittered invitingly behind them. 'There's a nice restaurant and I'm sure they'll have a kids' menu.'

Two pairs of green eyes stared back at her doubtfully, but Lydia was on a roll now, determined to end the day on a happier note, to somehow make up for her lacklustre feelings in the Bailey department.

'Come on, guys, it will be fun.'

At least it would have been, if Bailey hadn't knocked over a water jug the second they were seated, if he hadn't thrown a massive tantrum because the rolls the waiter produced had, heaven forbid, poppy seeds on top of them!

He's not mine, Lydia wanted to scream at the hundred faces that turned disapprovingly, and by the time they got around to reading the blessed menu Lydia's goodwill was evaporating as quickly as the waiter's humour as they waited for Bailey to choose.

'How about some yummy nuggets?' Lydia suggested. 'Or there are sausages and chips.'

'Just get him an ice cream.' Corey gave a tight shrug, handing the waiter back the menu.

'Cola!' Bailey added as the salt cellar went flying. So did Lydia's patience.

'And bring the sugar bowl, too,' she muttered as the waiter gratefully escaped.

'What's that supposed to mean?'

Biting back a smart reply, Lydia took a long sip of her drink.

'Now's hardly the time to be setting rules, Lydia,' Corey said, 'We're in a restaurant, for heaven's sake. I'd settle for not being the cabaret.'

Which wasn't the best start to what should have been a romantic evening.

Somehow they made it through dinner, declined dessert and didn't even bother with coffee.

'Lydia…' They were on the pavement. Bailey, now there wasn't an audience, was asleep on Corey's shoulders. The *Spirit of Tasmania*, the nightly ferry that carried Melbournians across the Tasman, glittered in the distance, ferrying its passengers to the Apple Isle. She stared at it because it was easier than staring at Corey, easier than seeing the disappointment in his eyes at the way the day had ended. 'I said it wouldn't be easy.'

'I know you did,' Lydia admitted, and suddenly she felt like crying. 'And I refused to listen to you. And instead of being nice, being supportive, I've been an absolute bitch.'

'No you haven't.' Corey almost laughed.

'I've ruined his day.'

'He's had a great day,' Corey insisted, but Lydia furiously shook her head. 'Hell, Lydia, if you knew what this kid has to put up with, you'd realise that today ranks up there with one of the best.'

Which made her feel worse, if that was possible.

'Let's get him home.'

Bailey slept in his car seat as Corey concentrated on the beach road, the hum of the radio in the background not quite filling the uncomfortable silence.

She watched as Corey gently carried the sleeping boy up the garden path of his parents' house, knowing this was a regular event—pyjamas after ten, different beds, different faces kissing him goodnight—and she wished, wished more than anything she had the energy to intervene, could summon the strength to like Bailey.

The silence as they drove back to Lydia's wasn't uncomfortable this time and even though he'd only stayed for one night already there was a comforting air of familiarity, an air of rightness as Lydia fumbled with the locks in the darkness, pushed open the door and flicked on the hall light.

'You look exhausted,' Corey commented as she padded through to the kitchen and automatically headed for the coffee-machine. 'Work will be a rest after today.'

'I'm just tired, that's all. It's par for the course at the moment,' she added, rubbing her back as Corey looked at her thoughtfully. 'I sound like such a moaner.'

'You don't.' Corey laughed but his voice grew more serious. 'I don't know how you do it, to tell the truth—on your feet most of the day and you don't have to tell me how impossibly hot it is in the unit.'

'It's just as hot for you.' Lydia shrugged. 'And I haven't run the length and breadth of the beach five hundred times, chasing a beach ball today.'

'But I'm not thirty-two weeks pregnant.' He gave a slow grin. 'I should go, let you get some sleep.' When Lydia didn't respond he went on tentatively, 'Or I suppose I could run you a bath.''

Lydia gave a slow smile. 'Well, don't just stand there.'

The warm water lapped on her tired aching body as Lydia wrestled with the day's events. She'd wanted so much for it to be perfect, wanted so much… Biting on her lower lip, it took a while to relax back, a while to let the water work its magic again as finally she admitted the truth. She wanted so much to care for Bailey.

She looked up as Corey appeared at the doorway, glass in hand.

'This should be champagne.'

'It should.' Lydia smiled. 'I'm thinking of having a bottle in an ice bucket as an incentive to push in the labour ward.'

Handing her the sparkling water, the glass slipped a fraction in her wet hands and Corey steadied it, his eyes working the length of her. Suddenly Lydia felt embarrassed at the ease with which she'd let him into her life, embarrassed for smiling seductively up at him, embarrassed for thinking her beached-whale pro-portions could ever be considered beautiful. But seeing the naked admiration in his eyes, something quelled the knot of tension.

'Room for one more?' Corey's voice was low and thick with lust, and as he slipped off his clothes Lydia felt her insides melt as he slid in beside her, clasping his slippery solid calves as he straddled her, almost hypnotically working the soap into a lather as he leant back and let out a long low sigh.

'Penny for them?' Lydia whispered.

'You'd need more than a penny.' His eyes were closed, the words just a murmur as Lydia massaged upwards, fingering a scar on his knee, frowning in concern as she traced the thick white line.

'What happened here?'

'Footy.' She felt more than saw him grin. 'Like I said at the café, I'm a "would've-been".'

'Meaning?'

'A knee reconstruction at sixteen doesn't exactly bode well for a career in footy, but according to Mum…' he gave a dry laugh '…and after a few beers, according to me, I could have made it.'

'Professionally?' Lydia checked, watching as he half nodded then lowering her lips to belatedly kiss away the hurt. 'So how did you end up nursing?' When he didn't answer straight away Lydia pressed on. 'It's a bit of a career move!'

'You're telling me!' Corey was clasping her thigh now, Corey making it terribly difficult to concentrate. 'When I had my knee op, about two a.m. one morning when the drugs were wearing off and it was an hour till my next painkiller, I kind of realised footy was over for me. I felt as if the world was over; then suddenly a nurse was sitting on the edge of the bed, pinching one of my chocolates and moaning about her money being stuck in one of the vending machines…' He smiled and Lydia realised she was smiling too, the scene so, so familiar. How many patients had she supposedly whiled the small hours away with? How many times, in happier days, had she chatted to a new mum or a confused dad about the idiosyncrasies of the cola machine in an attempt to gain a foothold, and she was grateful, so grateful that some unnamed nurse had taken the time to sit, to listen, to be there for Corey.

'Anyway…' Corey's sleepy voice dragged her back. 'We chatted, she made me laugh, told me I was way too young and good-looking to think the world had ended, and before I knew it my next painkiller was due, not just due but I was over by half an hour. And guess what?'

'You didn't need it?'

He nodded. 'Two paracetemol at six a.m. and I was up on crutches a couple of hours later. I knew there and then that if I couldn't play footy there was something else I could do, and suddenly nursing became an option.'

'What was her name? Lydia asked, knowing he would remember. Her soft smile widened as Corey answered.

'Doris.'

'I thought you were going to say Tiffany or Charlie…'

'Doris,' Corey said with a wicked smile. 'Built like a rugby player herself!'

'Come on, you.' He stood, pulling out the plug then grabbing a towel from the rail, slowly easing her out before wrapping her in it and leading her, exhausted, to bed.

And it was so blissful to slip between the sheets and have Corey holding her, Corey understanding that, as much as her body ached for him, tonight it needed sleep more.

'I think I love you, Lydia.'

His voice was a tentative stab in the dark and Lydia captured the hand on her shoulder, her eyes filling with tears as the enormity of their situation hit her.

'I think I love you too, but…' Her words strangled in a sob as his hand gripped hers tighter.

'Let's worry about the buts tomorrow,' Corey whispered, holding her close, massaging away her fears until sleep finally crept in. 'We're together tonight.'

CHAPTER EIGHT

'I'VE got DOC's on the phone.' Jo popped her head around the door of Corey's office. 'They say it's urgent.'

'Tell them I'll ring them back,' Corey answered without looking up. 'I'm on another call.'

Lydia barely registered the conversation, concentrating instead on Patrick's notes. A full meeting had been scheduled for three p.m. and she wanted to be prepared, running through the intricacies of his case with Corey, working out the nursing and social work issues, along with the medical ones. Unbelievably, the fact Corey had left her bed this morning didn't even get a look-in.

There was too much at stake.

Jenny, Patrick's mother, was still refusing to sign the consent form for his operation and a full legal battle was ensuing.

Having DOC's—the Department of Community Services—on the telephone was becoming an increasing regular event as Patrick struggled just to breathe.

'I can take it.' Lydia made to stand, but Jo shook her head.

'I think they wanted to speak to Corey.' Jo's voice was hesitant and something in the way she gave a wary shrug told Lydia not to push, something in the way Corey quickly finished his call and gave a tired nod told her it was bad news.

'Put them through.' There was a weary note of resignation, a tiny, dignified smile as he picked up the
phone.

'Corey Hughes.'

She tried to concentrate on her notes, tried to keep
an impassive expression, but hearing his ragged sigh,
the notes of exasperation creeping in, Lydia knew it
was a personal call. Quietly standing, she made to go,
but as she replaced the receiver, Corey called her back
just as she gripped the doorhandle.

'You don't have to leave.'

'It sounded personal.' Turning, she forced a bright
smile. 'I thought it might be easier if you were alone.'

'Nothing about this is easy.' She watched as he ran
a weary hand through his hair, then buried his face
in his hands, rubbing his eyes for a minute or two
before facing her. 'Adele's gone, or rather Adele
hasn't come back.'

'She's still in Queensland?' Lydia said, and Corey
nodded grimly.

'Apparently so.'

He picked up the stapler on his desk, stared at it
for a moment and then threw it across the room,
crashing it against the wall. Lydia stood there, tears
filling her eyes as she watched this beautiful strong
man visibly dissolve.

'She's not coming back.'

An awful silence ensued, one Lydia wanted to fill.

How she wished she could comfort him, could offer some insight, could somehow say the right thing.
But instead she stood there, staring somewhere between the stapler and the litter bin, trying to work out
what on earth she could say.

'I have to go.' It was Corey standing now, Corey setting the tone, making decisive movements, stuffing papers into his briefcase, pulling out the roster and running a finger along the endless list of names. 'I'll ask Joan to come in. She's up on Patrick's history, you can fill her in.'

'O-of course,' Lydia stammered.

'I'd better ring my mum, check that she's OK. I don't even know if she knows. What am I going to tell Bailey?'

Lydia shrugged helplessly. 'You don't have to tell him anything today. Maybe Adele will change her mind…'

'It's too late for that.' Corey dismissed her crumbs her comfort. 'DOC's have been watching her months now. She's been on her last chance for as long as can I remember and from the way they're talking, they mean business. They're talking about permanent foster-care, interim orders…' He raked a hand through his hair, dragged a long breath into his lungs and Lydia swore she could see a glimmer of tears in his eyes. 'Adele's really blown it this time.'

The phone started ringing about the same time as her pager started bleeping. Lydia clenched her teeth in frustration as Jo banged on the wall, urging her to come now. 'We'll talk later,' Lydia promised. 'As soon as I'm finished here I'll come over.'

'Your ultrasound appointment…' She watched his brow furrow. 'I could try and find—'

'I'll be fine,' Lydia broke in, ignoring her own stab of disappointment at the turn of events, knowing after what had just transpired an ultrasound appointment must surely be way down on his list. But as she turned and left, as she rushed out to the ward to face a barrage of decisions, for a tiny slice of time the implication of Adele's sudden departure started to hit home.

The day seemed to drag on for ever and though Lydia loved her work, though she stayed focused on the task in hand, knew she couldn't afford the luxury of a wandering mind, every moment was tempered with a need, a physical, aching need to be with Corey at this difficult time, to somehow comfort him, be there for him. But the special care unit afforded no such luxury. There wasn't even time to pick up the phone and check how he was doing, to let him know she was there for him, albeit in spirit only.

But, then again, what could she offer?

'Shouldn't you be somewhere else now?' Jo tapped at her watch, smiled as Lydia's brow furrowed. 'You've got an ultrasound appointment.'

Lydia gave a tense nod, picking up the phone with one hand as she tapped away on the computer with another. 'I just want to confirm Patrick's haemoglobin and potassium levels with the lab…'

'I can do that,' Jo offered, taking the telephone. 'Dr Reece's secretary just called to say that he's going to be here in an hour or so to reassess Patrick so why don't you nip downstairs, have your scan and then you'll be back in time to talk to him?'

Lydia didn't answer, just gabbled into the telephone, her worried nod confirming that the unsavoury results that had appeared on the screen were, in fact, correct. 'OK.' Lydia stood up, scribbling the IV orders as she did so. 'You know that Jenny's just rung through and wants the surgery to go ahead?'

She registered Jo's rather strained nod.

'If she rings again, or comes in I want to be paged. I've ordered some potassium to be added to his IV and the lab's going to ring when the packed cells are ready. His haemoglobin's dropped to seven so he needs an urgent transfusion.'

Jo nodded. 'I'll get straight onto it.'

'You'll ring me if there's any change?' Lydia asked.

'Of course,' Jo assured her. 'Come on, Lydia, you know that you need to have this scan. Your shift ended an hour ago.'

'Tell that to Patrick.' They walked back to the incubator, Jo relieving the nurse who had stood in for her toilet break as Lydia paused for a moment, not looking at the screens and endless tubes for once but at the little boy who she knew, just knew, wasn't going to make it.

'Can you believe that now Jenny's finally agreed to the operation, it's probably going to be too late? I can't see Dr Reece going ahead now, Patrick's just too sick,' Jo said sadly.

But as practical as ever, Lydia broke in. 'He's always been too sick, Jo. This isn't his mother's fault.'

'Isn't it?' They shared a sad smile, a tiny wistful look.

'Who knows what she's been through?' Lydia said softly. 'Who knows what's in her past? It isn't for us to judge Jo. We can't run people's lives for them, all we can do is try to pick up the pieces.'

'I know,' Jo agreed. 'But it doesn't stop it hurting.'

If ever Lydia had felt lonely before, it didn't compare to lying in the dark ultrasound room as the radiographer squeezed some jelly onto her stomach. Staring at the screen, she tried to concentrate, tried to summon up some passion for the life inside her, but it was too hard, too hard to focus when Corey wasn't here and Patrick lay so ill upstairs.

Too hard to contemplate that in a few short weeks she'd be leaving it all behind, for someone she didn't even know.

CHAPTER NINE

COREY'S flat was in darkness when finally Lydia
made it there. Seeing the hand on her clock edging
towards midnight, Lydia wrestled with whether to
knock, unsure of her reception, whether Corey would
appreciate the late night visit. But way more scary
than the lateness of the hour were her own dark
thoughts, whether, after an exhausting, emotionally
draining day, she was up to more dramas.

Was she really in a position to comfort him?

Not quite biting the bullet, she knocked gently, almost relieved when she got no response. Grappling
in her bag for a pen and some paper, shamefully
grateful at her temporary escape, Lydia fashioned a
quick note. But her relief was short-lived. The front
door opened and she stood like a rabbit caught in the
headlights, her pen guiltily poised over the paper. If
it had been under any other circumstances, her heart
would have melted at the sight of him. Dressed—if
you could call it that—in a pair of navy boxers, he
looked as untamed and sexy as she had ever seen him,
unshaven and tousled—and as exhausted as a man
could be and still remain standing.

'I—I thought you must be asleep,' she stammered.
'I didn't want to wake you.'

'I was in the laundry.' He shrugged, pulling the
door open further and gesturing for her to follow. 'I'm
on the first set of sheets for the night.'

Lydia had no idea what he was talking about, but followed him in, rambling her apologies as she did so. 'I would have called, I just didn't get the chance.'

'I understand,' Corey said, loading a pile of sheets into the washer and refusing to look at her.

'It really was horrendous today. If I could have got away any sooner…'

'I understand,' Corey said again, only this time he turned around. 'I work there, remember, I know what a hellhole it can be. What happened?'

Lydia didn't answer straight away, knowing his day had been bad enough, that the reason for her lateness would only add to his hell, but he answered his question for her.

'Patrick?'

Lydia gave a small nod.

'Is he…?' His voice trailed off and Lydia quickly jumped in.

'He's still alive.' She swallowed hard. 'But the operation's not going to happen. Jenny finally signed the consent form and everything, but he's gone further downhill. He simply wouldn't survive surgery.'

Corey gave a tight nod.

'I signed the DNR authority before I left.'

Her words hung in the air for a full minute and for Lydia it was the longest moment of her life. She felt like an executioner, the DNR authority the hardest she had done to date. The order not to resuscitate had been taken after long consultations with Drs Reece and Browne and finally Jenny. And though this decision was never taken lightly, although this was the right thing to do, putting pen to paper had been agony.

'How was your scan?' She heard his attempt at

cheerfulness, to shift the conversation away from tragic, but somehow she couldn't reciprocate.

'Normal.' Lydia shrugged. 'Everything seems to be fine.'

'So much for small talk.'

His words confused her and Lydia gave him a bemused look as he carried on talking.

'Most new couples are tossing up for the theatre or a meal at the weekend, and we've touched on a dying baby and your pregnancy…' She watched his Adam's apple bob a couple of times, tears stinging the back of her eyes as he carried on talking. 'And we haven't even touched the sides yet.'

'What happened today, Corey?'

He didn't answer at first, just added a slug of detergent to the washing machine then turned the dials.

'The inevitable happened.' He gave a wry smile but it didn't reach his eyes. 'I'll have to get some more sheets, the way Bailey goes through them…' He hesitated for a moment, not looking at her as he delivered his news. 'I'm applying for custody Lydia. I've got interim care for now.'

'Sole custody?' Lydia said, her heart stilling as Corey nodded. 'What about your parents? Surely they can—'

'They're in their sixties, Lydia. It isn't fair on them and it isn't fair on Bailey. It's me or foster-care and as hard as it's going to be, as much as I mightn't be ready for this, it's what I have to do. It's what I want to do,' Corey amended, but something in his stance told Lydia he was convincing himself as much as her.

It will be OK. How badly she wanted to say it, to walk over to him, to bury her head in his strong safe chest and tell him that everything would be fine, But instead she stood there frozen, the implications hitting home with frightening accuracy, painfully reiterated by Corey's direct voice.

'As of today I'm a father, Lydia. A father to a little boy with big problems. That's why I'm washing sheets at midnight. That's why I'm coming to work tomorrow to clear my desk before taking a few weeks off. And in that time I'll hopefully find us somewhere to live that isn't four storys high, given Bailey's disregard for danger. And while I'm at it I'll see if the kinder can up his hours and look for a day-care centre that can fill in the gaps while I go to work and attempt to earn enough to pay for it.'

He stared at her, his green eyes not so guarded now. Instead, they were almost defiant. 'I'm not selling myself very well here, am I, Lydia?' His biting sarcasm was like a slap to her pale cheeks. 'I'm not exactly painting a rosy picture for you, but that just about sums up my life at the moment. That's the way things are going to be for the foreseeable future and, no doubt, for a long while after. So, if you want to come along for the ride, it's your choice, but I can't afford passengers. Bailey's been messed around too long and too often to have someone waltz in, only to waltz out when the going gets too tough. Now, though I can't guarantee great company along the way, I can promise it will be hellishly bumpy.'

The washing machine chose that moment to growl in protest at its rather heavy load, thundering into noisy jerks that only served to exacerbate the tension as Corey thumped it into silence.

Maybe she should have said yes, maybe she should

have smiled bravely, said she was up to it, that she would do whatever it took to be beside him, but standing in a draughty laundry, drained, confused and quietly terrified at her own future, right there and then she couldn't do it, wasn't up to being brave.

This was a grown-up game with grown-up consequences. She simply couldn't afford the luxury of following her heart, there was too much at stake. And though it would have been so easy to say she was up to it, so much easier to walk towards him than to walk away, she was too raw, too vulnerable and too dammed scared to really believe that love would conquer all.

'I want to love him, Corey…'

'Love doesn't just happen, Lydia,' Corey said firmly, refusing to accept excuses.

'It did to us.' Confused eyes turned to his, becoming tear-laced as she watched him slipping away.

'He has to come first, Lydia, for me at least. That's the way it has to be. You've got a baby to think of. You don't need this now. I can't blame you for walking away.'

'I'm sorry, Corey.'

'You've nothing to be sorry for,' Corey said sadly. It's just too much, too soon, for both of us.'

She gave a small nod, words out of the question as her throat constricted against a fresh batch of tears as she turned to go.

'I'm sorry, too, Lydia. I promised I'd be there for you, promised I wouldn't let you down, and that's exactly what I've done.'

'You didn't know what was going to happen,' Lydia croaked, fumbling for the door, blinded by her tears. 'It's me that should be sorry. It's me being self-ish, me that wants all of you.'

'Love is out there, Lydia.' His words stopped her in her tracks, but she was too close to breaking down to turn around. 'Love is out there and one day it's going to happen for you. Some guy's going to come along and give you everything you need. Who knows? It might even happen for me.' He flashed a wry smile. 'Well, I'll keep my fingers crossed that in my case it's a woman.'

She managed a wobbly smile, grateful for the splash of humour in this dark, dark moment, but it changed midway and she started to cry again as his voice grew serious.

'I also know that in a different place, a different time we would have made it.'

She didn't respond, just closed the door on her tentative dreams, walked the lonely distance back to her car and sat for a full fifteen minutes before she could even consider starting the engine.

Exhausted and spent, she slipped into bed a little later, staring at the ceiling as the life within swooped and ducked beneath her hands.

Love is out there.

Corey's words filtered through her mind, brought on a fresh batch of tears.

Love was out there—so why had she chosen to go it alone?

CHAPTER TEN

WORK was hell.

Seeing Corey and knowing he was out of bounds, knowing she had pushed him away when he really needed her, was almost more than Lydia could take. Making their way around the incubators, discussing cases with Dr Browne, it took every inch of professionalism to keep her eyes from straying to Corey's as they reached Patrick's beside.

'His condition has deteriorated further since last night,' Lydia said in low tones, as Dr Browne waded through the notes, eyed the labs with knowing eyes before finally examining the infant.

'And the mother is sure she doesn't want to see him?' Dr Browne asked. Lydia bit on her lower lip as she nodded, bit so hard it actually hurt as Dr Browne carried on speaking. 'I think we all know that we've come to the end of the road with Patrick, that the decision has nothing to do with his handicaps. Quite simply his body's had enough, there is nothing modern medicine can do to prolong his life.' He gave a small cough, the only indication of the effect this conversation was having on him. It hit Lydia then how it really did affect them all. That whether you blurted it out or kept it firmly locked in, this job got to everyone. 'Does anyone have any questions?'

No one did. Everyone present knew that this was

one battle that simply couldn't be won, their only comfort that everything possible had been attempted.

'I suggest someone senior explains the situation once again to Patrick's mother, but I feel it would be inappropriate to prolong this baby's life in the hope that his mother comes around. The patient has to come first.' He gave a small nod, moved on to the next incubator, and the rest of the staff followed.

Lydia didn't catch up with Corey till later, much later—long after his shift had ended, long after they both should have been at home.

'Did you arrange your leave?'

She was hovering by his office door, hoping for a brief chat, for anything other than the strained silence that had followed them since last night.

'All sorted.' He flashed a smile she knew was false. 'Well, not really. I've given myself Christmas off, which didn't go down too well, but I figure Bailey deserves to have me home and given that I've worked the last eight Christmases, Admin didn't really have a leg to stand on.'

'Christmas!' Lydia gave a low laugh, but more to herself. She'd almost forgotten that Christmas was just around the corner. The staff notices appearing on the board, inviting the team to meals, drinks, parties, just somehow didn't seem to apply to her. Her mind flashed back to last year, when everything had seemed safe and good, when trust and love had still been in her life.

'Lydia!' Jo came over, a note of anxiety in her voice. 'Patrick's obs have deteriorated.'

Lydia didn't answer, just followed her colleague over to the incubator with a heavy heart. She had known this moment was coming, had supposedly mentally prepared herself for it, but now that it was here, she realised how woeful her preparations had been, and from the look on Corey's face when he joined them a few moments later he was just as unprepared.

'I just rang Jenny.'

'Is she coming?' Lydia knew the answer before he even shook his head.

'She said to let us know when it's over.'

Lydia gently examined the babe, not wanting to cause distress or perform unnecessary procedures but equally determined to alleviate any pain or suffering if at all possible. Most of the equipment had been removed now. Only a single IV line remained, along with the monitors recording his observations. Alarms were being triggered as Patrick's blood pressure plummeted.

'He seems comfortable.' Lydia pulled a bunny rug around his tiny shoulders, placed a tender hand on his little forehead as she spoke. 'Let me know if he gets distressed, but I think now might be the time to take all the monitors off. There's nothing more we're going to do unless he's uncomfortable.'

'I'm just going to make a phone call home.' Corey's voice was thick, the muscles on his face quilted with the effort of keeping emotion in check. 'Then could one of you bring Patrick to me in the side room?'

Lydia closed her eyes for a fraction of a second before turning them on Corey. The side room was named that because no one on God's earth could come up with another name for it. It was a pretty pastel-colored room, with a Moses basket, murals on the wall, and under any other circumstances it would have been beautiful.

But how could one like a room where a lifetime of love and cuddles had to be crammed into a few short minutes or hours, a room where parents got to hold their baby, maybe for the first time but always for the last.

'You don't have to do this, Corey. It could be ages till he…' She shook her head briefly, frustrated at her poor attempts, sure her words had sounded too harsh, too remote, but she simply couldn't bear to see Corey drag himself through the mill in the name of duty, pour emotion onto emotion. He'd been through enough, and as he stalked back to his office she followed him, dodging the closing door and facing him head on. 'What I'm trying to say…' Her voice trailed off but after swallowing hard she found it again. 'What I'm trying to say is that it might be too much for you.'

'Just because you like leaving when the going gets tough, Lydia, it doesn't mean we all have to work that way.'

'That's unfair,' Lydia retorted, her eyes brimming with hurt and tears. 'You can't compare this to what's happened to us.'

'Oh, can't I?' Corey's look was pure venom. 'You go home, Lydia. It's been a long day. You go home and put your feet up.'

'Who said anything about going home? Patrick's my patient and I'll sleep in the on-call room in case I'm needed, all night if I have to. Just because I can't do what you do, just because I can't lay myself on the line, it doesn't make me cold-hearted, Corey. I may not wear my heart on my sleeve but it's still beating.'

Her words must have reached him for the anger seemed to leave him, the fire went out of his voice. He looked older suddenly, older and more tired but infinitely beautiful. 'I was out of line,' he apologised. 'I know you care, Lydia, just as much as I do. We just have different ways of showing it, that's all. Personally, it's easier for me to stay.'

'You do what gets you through, Corey.' The row was over but his words had stung and Lydia wasn't prepared to just let it all go without comment. Turning for the door, she paused a moment. 'And just in case you still think this is easy for me…' She gave a disbelieving laugh. 'Believe me, Corey, sometimes the hardest part is walking away.'

She lay in the on-call room, eyes wide open, staring at the ceiling and wishing she could go to him, wishing she was one of those strong people that could be counted on.

Maybe there *was* a fundamental difference between doctors and nurses, Lydia mused when around two a.m. the night sister called her and she walked to the side room. She could make all the tough calls—sign the DNR order, request the removal of monitors, perform the necessary examinations as Corey held him gently, even certify a little life extinct at two-twelve a.m.—but when push came to shove, as awful as it was for Lydia, Corey was the one doing the tough task.

'Are you going home now?' Lydia wrote on the notes, offered a prayer in her head and then headed for the door.

'In a while.' Corey gently placed the babe in the Moses basket. 'I'm going to make a memory box for Jenny. Maybe one day she'll need it.'

Lydia didn't answer, closed the door softly, before picking up her bag and heading for the car park.

There was a difference, she decided.

It was the nurses who really laid their hearts on the line.

CHAPTER ELEVEN

LYDIA loathed her antenatal appointments. Hated sitting in the crowded waiting room with dewy-eyed couples all eyeing her suspiciously as she sat conspicuously alone in her theatre blues. But then again she loathed everything at the moment.

Loathed a world without Corey.

Still, being a doctor on call had some compensations and invariably the receptionist would give her a wink and shuffle her notes to the top of the queue.

'How many weeks now, Dr Verhagh?' Shirley asked brightly as a blushing Lydia handed over her specimen wrapped in a tissue, wishing they made the jars opaque. Even the fact she was a doctor was no barrier against the general lack of dignity pregnancy entailed.

Three, Lydia nearly answered.

Three awful weeks since she had last seen Corey.

Three weeks of reaching for the telephone then shrinking away, three weeks of crying herself to sleep and waking up in tears.

But, of course, that wasn't what Shirley was asking.

'Thirty-five,' Lydia replied instead, pulling out her diary as Shirley ran her finger down the appointment list.

'Which means Dr Hamilton will want to see you weekly from now on. Would you like the same time next Wednesday?' She pulled a face. 'Actually, Wednesday's a bit full.'

'Any day will do,' Lydia said amicably. 'I go on maternity leave at the end of this week, so put me in whenever.'

'Thursday at ten? 'Shirley checked, pencilling it in then giving a wide-eyed look to the examination room down the corridor and not too subtly jerking her head in its general direction. 'Now, Dr Hamilton has a medical student with him today, so if you've any objections to the student being present, just let me know.'

Lydia shook her head. 'That's fine.' Though the very last thing she wanted was an audience, Lydia was hardly in a position to object! She'd been a medical student herself, had prodded and poked in the name of education, even huffed that it was a teaching hospital when the patient had exercised their right to refuse!

'Go to exam room one,' Shirley whispered as Lydia gave her a grateful nod of thanks. 'They shouldn't be too much longer,'

'Good morning, or should I say good afternoon?' Dr Hamilton beamed, uncharacteristically clapping his hands together and making jolly small talk as Lydia clambered up onto the examination couch. 'Hamish will be watching today as Shirley hopefully explained. Now, how are we feeling?'

'Fine,' Lydia answered as he listened to her blood pressure, bewildered at the change in Dr Hamilton, then realising the display was entirely for the benefit of his student. 'Well, a bit tired but that's to be expected.'

'And are we getting excited?'

No, Lydia was tempted to answer, but didn't have the energy or heart to break the rather jolly atmosphere with her lethargic misgivings. 'I'm sure once my maternity leaves start I'll believe it's really happening,' she responded somewhat lamely instead.

'Oh, it's happening,' Dr Hamilton boomed, laughing at his own weak joke before speaking over her to Hamish. 'Dr Verhagh works on the special care unit, though not for much longer,' he added, indicating for Lydia to pull up her top and examining her bump carefully. 'Do you mind if Hamish checks the position?'

Lydia nodded her consent and closed her eyes, trying to ignore the awkward probing hands of the student as he attempted to locate the baby's position, fumbling for what seemed an inordinate amount of time before declaring that the baby was indeed head down, then qualifying it with a rather weak, 'I think.'

'Excellent,' Dr Hamilton agreed, 'and while this baby appears on the small side, all the scans show that it's well within normal limits. That's quite a neat little package you've got there! Now, if you'd like to slip on a gown, Dr Verhagh, we'll see about taking some swabs.'

Lydia groaned inwardly, cringing at the false friendliness, preferring instead Dr Hamilton's normally brusque bedside manner. If her stomach was a neat little package, what on earth was he going to say when she took her knickers off?

'I like to test for strep B between thirty-five and thirty-seven weeks gestation,' Dr Hamilton explained as Hamish scribbled furiously on his notepad. 'It's a simple swab, a routine test, and though the mother may produce no symptoms, many women, in fact, carry the bacterium with no ill effect; however, if it's transmitted to the baby during labour, the results can be devastating. If the mother produces a positive result, can you remember the treatment I outlined?'

Hamish clearly couldn't and the longest pause ensued as Lydia lay there wishing both men could resume this conversation elsewhere and let her get undressed.

'A Caesarean section?' Hamish finally responded, blushing furiously as Dr Hamilton shook his head.

'IV antibiotics during labour,' he corrected. 'Strep B infection is one of the leading causes of infection and death in neonates and the simple administration of IV antibiotics during labour is the only necessary treatment. Worth remembering, I'd say,' Dr Hamilton added rather edgily, his façade slipping. 'We'll leave Dr Verhagh to get changed and I'll set up for the swab.'

She wasn't in the mood for this. Shirley had said nothing about swabs. If she'd known this was happening today, Lydia would have arranged her appointment for early morning. Instead, she was five hours into a hot shift with unshaven legs and had the gormless Hamish watching, to boot.

It was a relief when her pager went off.

'Nothing urgent, I hope.' Dr Hamilton said as Lydia poked her head around the curtain.

'I'm not sure,' Lydia lied, 'but I am needed back on the unit. Can this wait till next week?'

'Can it?' Dr Hamilton looked over to Hamish who blushed deeper, if that was possible.

'The protocol suggests between thirty-five and thirty-seven weeks gestation, so...'

'It will keep,' Dr Hamilton agreed. 'But be sure and prompt me next week if I forget, Dr Verhagh.'

'Will do,' Lydia agreed, shaking hands as she hurriedly left the office and headed for the unit.

'Jackie Gibb is here to see you,' Joan, the assistant unit manager greeted Lydia as she swept onto the ward. 'The other half of your job share! She thought it might be nice to catch up before you went off on maternity leave.'

Lydia couldn't decide if her escape had been quite as lucky as she entered the staffroom.

Suddenly a swab seemed preferable to the woeful feelings of inadequacy that swept over her as a tanned, slim Jackie greeted her. She epitomised sophistication—a smart boxy suit, slim legs crossed at the ankles, hair neatly tied into a smart chignon, the antithesis of a rather dishevelled, slightly breathless Lydia

'Dr Verhagh,' Jackie said warmly. 'Forgive me if I don't stand.' She gestured to the tiny infant, which Lydia hadn't even noticed, wrapped in navy cashmere, feeding unobtrusively, and even though it was terribly politically incorrect, even though it had never bothered her before, suddenly Lydia felt terribly uncomfortable. Which was ridiculous, Lydia mentally scolded herself, trying not to blush and look Jackie in the eye at the same time as they discussed the intricacies of job sharing. She saw women breastfeed every day. It was the most natural thing in the world, she'd be doing it herself soon!

But, a tiny voice said, would she be doing it with such style?

'I hope you don't mind me landing on you.' Jackie smiled after picking Lydia's brains for the best part of an hour. 'I just thought it might make things a bit easier if we touched bases before we swap over. Dr Browne's team is on call this weekend so it's nice to be reasonably up to date with the patients before I dive back in. I'm going to come in on Friday and join you for the ward round. I like to be organised.'

'Of course,' Lydia said, heaving herself off the rather low sofa as Jackie stood up smartly and placed her incredibly placid baby into its carry seat. 'I was actually going to come in on Saturday morning and go over things with you, so you've saved me a trip,' Lydia lied. She'd been going to do no such thing, but she certainly didn't want Jackie to know that!

'You can have lie-in instead. Well, it's been lovely meeting you, Lydia. I might just pop around and show Declan off to the nurses. I'd like to have a word with Corey too, if he's on duty.'

'He's off at the moment.' Lydia fiddled with her pen. 'I think he comes back next week, though.'

'Thank heavens for that.' Jackie rolled her sparkling, well made-up eyes. 'I can't stand the place when he isn't around. Now, once you're back...' Jackie flashed a perfectly capped smile '...if you have any problems with the roster, just ring me at home.' She pressed a card into Lydia's hand. 'I'm more than happy to fill in at short notice. Can't have the nanny twiddling her thumbs, now, can we?'

Maybe money did buy happiness, Lydia mused as she watched Jackie's trim backside depart.

Maybe if she had enough money to afford a nanny and a personal trainer and no doubt a housekeeper, then she'd be as jolly and gorgeous and efficient as Jackie, but as she rounded the corner, dreaming of the impossible slipped away as her heart skipped into overdrive at the sight of Corey, casual in jeans and a T-shirt but with an air of authority that could never be dimmed.

Oh God, she hadn't prepared herself for this! Had almost convinced herself that the next time she saw him she'd be slim and gorgeous, a sort of clone of the perfect Jackie! Instead, she stood with a shiny red face, forcing a smile as she tried to think of an excuse for a hasty retreat while Jackie greeted him like a long lost friend.

'I've just been catching up with Lydia.' Jackie beamed, dragging her reluctantly into the conversation. 'She told me you weren't due back.'

'That was the plan.' Corey gave a rueful smile. 'I'm in for a couple of hours a day this week to do some paperwork, but I'll be back properly on Monday.'

'Well, I'll look forward to seeing you then,' Jackie said, catching the eye of one of the nurses and waving frantically before disappearing in a cloud of perfume.

They stood for an awkward moment, the silence growing around them.

'You look well,' Corey said finally, when it was clear someone had to say something.

'I actually felt well until I met…' Lydia bit hard on her lip, not wanting Corey to add *bitchy* to her list of negative attributes, but he read her like a book.

'A little bird tells me Jackie had two weeks in

Queensland at a health retreat,' Corey said. 'The baby
slept down the hall with the nanny.'

'Oh!' Lydia blinked, a smile breaking out on her
strained face.

'Anyway, you look wonderful.' He gave a small
embarrassed cough and Lydia did the same.

'How are things with you?' The tensions that had
abated a smidgen with the idle chat about Jackie suddenly quadrupled as Lydia crossed some invisible
line.

'Getting there,' Corey said vaguely.

'And Bailey?' Lydia pressed on, desperate for
some insight, to find out how things were working
out, for though she'd signed herself out, her heart was
still with him. But the subject was clearly out of
bounds. Corey didn't even attempt a polite answer,
just shook his head and shot her a warning look with
his eyes. 'I'd best get on.'

And get on he did.

The occasional glimpse of his broad shoulders
hunched over his office desk was the only luxury afforded as Lydia struggled through her last days of
work.

There came a time in pregnancy, however vehemently
opposed, however much you wanted to keep going,
that your body simply said enough, and for Lydia it
came on the final Friday. Heaving herself out of bed
and staggering into the shower, Lydia waited for the
water to work its magic, even turned the cold tap up
higher, hoping the icy jets would somehow invigorate
her, but all to no avail. Even dressing was a chore.
Eyeing the rumpled sheets, a legacy of yet another

sleepless night, she was tempted, sorely tempted to say to hell with the world, to climb right back in and hibernate a while.

A flat car battery, courtesy of leaving the lights on overnight, accentuated her gloom, but the mental image of Jackie, crisp and raring to go, of Dr Browne glancing at his watch and muttering under his breath, was enough incentive to have Lydia fumbling for the local taxi number and pleading to jump the queue.

'Maternity unit?' The driver asked as she attempted to pull the seat belt around her bump.

'Just the main entrance, thanks.' Lydia smiled then pointedly stared out of the passenger window, too tired for idle chatter.

Oh, she ached, every part of her body seemed to be crying for her to stop. Even her brain seemed to have slowed down, so much so that if it hadn't been for Jackie's presence the ward round would have taken for ever.

'Why don't you call it a day?' Jackie perched her pretty little bottom on the nurses' station desk as Lydia attempted to focus on the screen in front of her. 'I'm more than happy to cover for you.'

'I'm fine,' Lydia said through gritted teeth, determined not to lower her guard and wishing Jackie would just leave her alone. 'I'm just a bit tired, that's all.'

Jackie let out an annoyingly pretty laugh. 'Well, you're doing better than I did. My last two weeks here Jo had to practically wheel me around in a wheelchair and most of my time was spent in a crumpled heap at the nurses' station, crying my eyes out over Dr Browne's latest insensitive remark.'

Lydia looked up sharply, her eyes narrowing disbelievingly. 'But Dr Browne's been nothing but understanding…'

'Because I threatened to report him for sex discrimination. We had to go to mediation, can you imagine?' Jackie took a deep breath and for the first time Lydia looked, really looked at the woman who was sitting next to her; finally saw the heavily made-up eyes covering dark hollows, the lines of tension around her pouting lips.

'You just seem so…' Lydia chewed on her lip, unsure how far she could go here, not quite convinced she could trust her nemesis. 'So in control. So assured.'

'Well, if you're convinced, hopefully I've fooled Dr Browne. But if you really want the truth, my boobs are killing me.' She gave a tight smile. 'My jaw's aching from smiling and it feels as if everyone's talking a different language.

'Go home,' she added softly. 'And when you come back, we can lean on each other.' She smiled at Lydia's disbelieving look. 'Why do you think I was so quick to give you my phone number? Why do you think I'm shooing you out the door now?' When Lydia didn't answer, Jackie carried on talking. 'I'm storing up favours, that's why. Storing them up in the hope that when my nanny ups and leaves or Declan's got a doctor's appointment or whatever the latest drama is, I can call on you.'

'You can.' Lydia met Jackie's eyes for the first time.

'And you can call on me, too.'

'I'm starting to think this might actually work.'

'It has to' Jackie said. 'We've worked too hard to topple off the ladder now. Do you know why women work ten times harder than a man to get anywhere, Lydia? Why women have the babies and juggle a career as well as a home?'

Lydia gave a brief shrug, simply not up to a feminist, sister-to-sister lecture.

'Because we can.'

Lydia blinked a couple of times as Jackie's words filtered through.

'Remember that, Lydia.' Standing up, she reinstated her pearly smile. 'I'll just let Corey know you're heading off so he can summon the troops.'

'Summon the troops.' Lydia gave a bemused frown, watching as Jackie strode off, realisation only dawning as Corey came out of his office dragging an obscenely large basket behind him wrapped in Cellophane and tied with a huge yellow bow.

And even though she'd put more dollars into more brown envelopes than she could even begin to remember, never, not even for a moment had Lydia thought the same was being done for her. Even at her old hospital her parting had been so hasty it had barely registered a blip, yet suddenly here she was the reluctant centre of attention, holding in tears that would surely be shed later, as her new colleagues and almost friends wished her all the luck in the world for her journey ahead.

'Up on the wards,' Corey spoke across the unit, his deep voice carrying as every eye looked on, 'this would be done in the staffroom, but here on Special Care we can't afford the luxury of slipping away for five minutes, here on Special Care we need to organise a replacement just to arrange a toilet break, so when it comes time to say goodbye, it has to be done on the shop floor.' He paused for a moment, waiting patiently as Jo fiddled with a monitor, checked her small charge and proved his point entirely. 'All right, Jo?' Corey checked, only resuming his speech when Jo gave the thumbs-up. 'So we say our goodbyes in front of the parents and babies which seems more fitting somehow, because here more than anywhere it's not just the patients' lives we're involved in, but the families', too.

'Lydia has only been here a short time, but already she's shown us what a fabulous doctor she is and how lucky we are to have her on board. It goes without saying that more than a few parents present today will remember Lydia for ever, remember how her skills saved their baby's life.'

'Hear, hear,' Meredith called out, and the tears that had been threatening seemed precariously close as Corey cleared his throat and paused for a moment. Lydia would have looked at her feet if her bump had allowed so instead she looked down as Corey carried on talking. 'We all wish Lydia well, all wish for a healthy, happy baby.' He gave a soft laugh. 'And while we're at it, let's all wish for an incredibly easy birth. Good luck, Lydia.'

And then it was over. Sick babies stopped for no one and it was left to Lydia to locate a wheelchair, heave the basket up onto it and blurt out a few farewells as she made her way to the lift. And if Corey hadn't been there, if Corey hadn't been pressing the button just as she arrived, she might even have made it without breaking down.

'Are you OK?' The concern in his voice was genuine but she could hear the guarded note as the lift doors closed behind them.

'Just tired.' Lydia shrugged, rummaging in her pocket for a handkerchief. 'Tired and a bit emotional, I guess.'

'You're allowed to be.' He gestured to her bump before focusing on the lift buttons. 'Do you need a hand to get this into the car?'

'My car died this morning. I'm getting a taxi.'

'I'll give you a lift.'

Lydia shook her head. 'I'll be fine.'

'Lydia.' His hand caught her arm as she attempted to guide the wheelchair down the polished corridor. 'I can give you a lift home, for heaven's sake. Is it so bad between us I can't even do that for you?'

'Of course not,' Lydia gulped, but it was all she could manage. Watching him loading the basket was too painfully reminiscent of their night at the ball, too reminiscent of when the world had held so much promise, to allow for much else.

Ever the gentleman, he carried the basket to the front door, stood for an uncomfortable moment as she located her keys. 'Do you want to come in, for a coffee or something…?' Her voice petered out, knowing it was the last thing either of them needed now.

'Better not. I've got to collect Bailey from kindergarten.' He was jiggling his keys in his pocket, looking out somewhere beyond her right shoulder. 'Lydia, I really do wish you all the best, I really do…'

'Don't.' Screwing her eyes closed, Lydia put up a

shaking hand. 'I made it through your speech at work, but I don't think I could be so brave the second time around.'

'You have to be,' Corey said gently, 'because that was my NUM speech and this one's from me. Just because it's over between us it doesn't stop me from caring, Lydia. I am here for you, if you need me.'

She nodded, looked him in the eye as she spoke. 'How's Bailey?' As the shutters came down she pushed on regardless. 'It works both ways, Corey. If we're going to work together, admit that we still care for each other, we have to be able to speak about the things that matter.'

He gave a weary nod. 'Bailey's getting there.' There was a note of fondness and pride in his voice that she'd never heard before. 'Actually, he's doing really well. We're going to repeat his kinder year, which will hopefully give him a chance to catch up and the courts are pushing things through and if all goes to plan it will be made legal in time for Christmas.' His eyes held hers. 'Which is what I want.'

'Then I'm happy for you.'

He held her then, held her against him, brushing her salty cheeks with his lips. And it felt so right, so utterly, utterly right to be in his arms, to be wrapped in the safe cocoon of his embrace, that not for the first time Lydia wondered how she could have let him go.

'Maybe we could—' she started, but he silenced her with his finger, stopping her with one gentle touch.

'Don't make promises you can't keep, Lydia.' Those delicious green eyes were swimming with tears as he reluctantly let her go. 'Don't make promises when you're drunk on emotion and too tired to think straight. Maybe you should get some rest, think things over before you say something you might regret...'

She nodded dumbly, stood there as he opened the door for her, stepped inside and watched him leave.

CHAPTER TWELVE

THE bed she had fantasised about all day didn't live up to expectations. Lying on top in her nightie, the room impossibly hot, Lydia tried to shut out the ridiculous conundrums that kept popping into her head, begged sleep to come and put an end to the ridiculous thoughts she was having.

Maybe she could do it!

Maybe she could be a mother of two.

With a surge of energy that surprised even Lydia, she stood up, pacing the floor, nibbling furiously on her thumbnail, the lethargy that had plagued her all day a distant memory now as a million jumbled thoughts cluttered her brain, vying for space, tossing up questions that Lydia equally rapidly answered.

They could live here!

Corey could sell his apartment, and they could all live here! Walking out to the hallway, she gazed across the landing at the three empty bedrooms with mounting excitement. Corey could do some night shifts, they could juggle their rosters…. The backache that had plagued her all day upped a notch and Lydia gripped the banister, breathing out slowly as the pain eased off, before resuming her incessant pacing. For the hell of it she grabbed a cloth and wiped down the vanity unit, fuelled by the plans that were really starting to take shape.

So it would be hard but, hell, life *was* hard sometimes. Even the gorgeous Jackie admitted she struggled.

Wiping down the tiles around the sink, Lydia eyed them critically, digging into the grouting with her cloth, then with a flash of inspiration pulled an old toothbrush out of the vanity unit, furiously scrubbing the grouting as she put the world to rights.

They really could make it work.

Catching sight of herself in the mirror, even Lydia managed to laugh. What on earth did she look like? Heavily pregnant, scrubbing the tiles with a toothbrush in her nightie. Anyone would think she was in labour or something!

And she would have laughed on, would have seen the funny side, if only a sudden trickle down her leg hadn't ruined the vaguely funny joke.

There was no need to rush.

Lydia knew that. Knew that even though her waters had broken there was no need to panic, that nothing was going to suddenly happen, but a knot of panic, a bubble of excitement started to well within her at the sheer inevitability of it all.

Call the hospital!

Dialling the number, chatting to the midwife, Lydia felt curiously deflated at the lack of urgency in the midwife's voice.

Her waters had broken, for goodness' sake!

The baby was on its way!

She hadn't expected a fanfare, the midwife to scream down the telephone in jubilation, but a touch of euphoria wouldn't go amiss!

OK, so maybe her contractions weren't going to start tonight. Maybe she should do as the midwife suggested and check her bag, make a cup of tea, even lie down and get some rest. Heaven knew, she'd need her energy later. But she was having a baby, for goodness' sake. How on earth was she supposed to relax?

The violence of her first contraction caught Lydia unawares, like a tight belt gripping around her lower abdomen, pulling tightly, pushing down into her lower back with such strength Lydia leant on the bedhead for a moment, involuntarily holding her breath, only to release it in a short sharp burst when the pain blissfully subsided.

The bubble of panic that had started to well was multiplying rapidly now. If that was just the start of labour, what the hell would she be like at the end? If that was mild, what the hell was a strong one going to do to her?

A wave of something akin to guilt washed over her as she remembered her own time as a junior doctor in the labour ward, the unspoken but probably tangible assumption that surely it couldn't be that bad, surely there was no need to scream *that* loudly.

How on earth was she going to get through this? How was she supposed to do this alone?

There wasn't exactly time to dwell on the answer? Just as she made it to the bookshelf, just as she pulled down her rather well-thumbed book of obstetrics and located the soothing pages of a first-time labour, another contraction gripped her. This time as she felt her thighs start to involuntarily quiver, felt her teeth grind together as she willed it to pass, Lydia knew there and then that there was no way she was going to last the requisite twenty-four hours, no chance of doing this and surviving into the night and for the rest of tomorrow.

The baby was on its way.

It *did* enter her head to ring the hospital again, but as paranoia started to creep in she could almost hear the midwives laughing. 'Pain? She thinks that's painful?' Lydia thought of ringing her mother, but she was on the other side of Melbourne. Even with traffic permitting, she'd be looking at the best part of an hour. As an another contraction gripped her, as the effort to push suddenly overwhelmed her, Lydia knew she had to pick up the phone, get help, and quickly. But even though the emergency number was ingrained in her mind, even though it would be the sensible option, even though she'd signed herself out of Corey's life, as she dialled his number and waited for him to pick up, Lydia was past caring about the sensibility of her decision.

She needed him.

Needed him beside her, needed him here now.

Reason didn't get a look-in.

'Corey speaking.'

How normal his voice sounded, how utterly, utterly normal. Swallowing a scream, she somehow managed to gasp into the phone, gritting her teeth in the effort of not pushing.

'I'm having it.'

'Lydia?' She heard the incredulity in his voice, heard the pause as he waited for normal services to resume, for her to tell him she was joking, that her waters had just broken, that there was ages to go yet. She was vaguely aware of him calling to Bailey, shouting at him to put something down, and as her contraction faded it was a slightly breathless Lydia who finally spoke, wondering in bemusement if she was imagining things.

'My waters broke,' she gasped.

'You've got ages yet,' Corey said reassuringly. 'Just because you're waters have broken, it doesn't mean anything's about to happen.'

'What if I bloody want to push?' Lydia screamed, clutching the phone as she sank to the floor, rocking on her heels and willing it to end. 'What then?' she sobbed when finally it was over.

'Have you called an ambulance?' She could hear the urgency in his voice but was beyond reassuring him.

'I was going to, but I called you instead.'

'I'm leaving now.' Corey's voice was sharp. 'I'm on my way. *I'll* call the ambulance.'

'What do I do?'

For a second she heard the humour in his voice, for a fraction of time she even smiled as his voice winged its way down the line.

'I'll tell you what to do—don't push till I get there.'

Which was all very well for *him* to say. All very well for *him* to tell her not to push. *He* wasn't the one with a freight train running through his body, *he* wasn't the one with his foot stuck on the accelerator and all the stations rushing past at lightning speed, *he* wasn't the one who wanted to pull the emergency stop cord and get off right this very minute.

But he was the one she *needed*.

Never had the sound of a car screeching to a halt sounded more welcome, never had the sound of pounding footsteps running up the drive been better received.

She could hear him guiding Bailey into the lounge, with barely a pause before running up the stairs and joining her in the bedroom and even though she must have looked a sight, she didn't care. The whole neighborhood could have marched in for ringside seats and Lydia wouldn't have batted an eyelid.

Corey was here, she could finally let go.

'Where's the hot water?' He grinned and even Lydia managed a laugh as Corey crouched down before her.

'I don't possess a kettle.'

It gripped her then, a need, an urge. However the books described it, it didn't come close to the primitive force that overwhelmed her, the utter and inexplicable desire to push, to grit her teeth and bear down, to push, to force, expel, all wrapped up in the scream that reverberated through her body, drawing on the strength of the shoulders she leant on, the arms she squeezed, nails digging into his flesh as Mother Nature set to work, a tiny life squeezing its way into the world guided by the loving hands of Corey.

His presence her constant.

'I want it to stop,' Lydia sobbed, utterly spent, utterly, utterly exhausted. 'I can't do this!'

'Yes, Lydia, you can.' His eyes locked on hers. His hands guided hers down to the soft damp curls of her infant, steadying her like a life raft in a storm, reminding her of the reason for the agony, the tangible proof, if ever she'd needed it, that this was a life she bringing into the world.

'I don't know if I'm ready...' The fear, the doubt

in her voice was genuine, and for a tiny slice of time he moved his attention away from all that was unfolding, dragged her into his arms as she sobbed onto his shoulders. 'I don't know if I'm ready to be a mum.'

'You're ready, Lydia, and what's more—you're going to be wonderful.'

And suddenly it was here, her hands, his hands intermingled, guiding, pulling, embracing the miracle of creation as Lydia's piercing scream filled the evening air, mingling with the wail of sirens, overtaken in a moment by the lusty cries of her newborn, barely noticing the paramedics who raced into the confined space of her bedroom, wrapping a blanket around her as she focused, just focused on the delicious, intoxicating sight of her daughter, scarcely able to comprehend that the pink, warm, alive body, rigid with anger, shocked and furious at her rapid entry to the world, only stilled, only hushed when, guided by the strong hands of Corey, she curved into her mother and latched on. Lydia gazed on in wonder, scarcely able to believe she was calming, consoling, nursing her own baby, that she had stilled those furious tears, that she was what this baby needed. In that moment alone Lydia became a mother.

'She's beautiful,' Lydia sobbed, her eyes drinking her in, breathing her in, living her, loving her, marvelling at the glorious pink of her fists, the knowing, curious eyes that locked on hers with a recognition that burnt into her soul.

'You were wonderful.' Corey's eyes were on the baby but his words were directed at Lydia. 'You were so wonderful.'

'So were you!' Her eyes never left her child but tears laced her words. 'I shouldn't have called you, it wasn't fair of me, but I didn't know what else to do.'

'You were right to call.' He was kissing her hair, pulling her into the safest, warmest of embraces. 'It was right I was here.'

'Was it?' Her eyes met his then, only briefly, a little lady demanding too much attention to allow for more. 'You understand?'

'I understand.' His words were soft but strong, and she leant on him, allowed herself the decadence of his embrace for a stolen moment before the paramedic gently loaded her onto the stretcher, the baby still wrapped in her warm arms.

'I'd better check on Bailey.' Corey's smile was almost apologetic. 'He hasn't a clue what's going on.'

'I'm sorry.' Suddenly reality was starting to sink in. 'He must have been terrified.

'It wouldn't have touched sides—he's too used to wild parties.' Corey's eyes were distinctly misty. 'But can I bring him in?' Corey swallowed hard. 'If you say no, I'll understand. I'm just trying to explain things to him, trying to—'

'That's fine,' Lydia said bravely, but all semblance of holding back vanished as Corey led a bewildered little guy into the room, watching his guarded, mistrusting face break into a smile as he glimpsed the pink, sweet face cradled in her arms.

'Baby!' His delight, the shrill euphoria of his squeal touched her soul, not even flinching as chubby fingers reached towards the soft dark down of her baby's hair.

'Just look, mate,' Corey said softly, but Lydia just smiled.

'You can stroke her cheek, Bailey,' she said softly. 'It's a baby, you're right. That's why I was shouting, but there was nothing to be scared of.' Her eyes locked on his and her heart seemed to melt again. Corey's eyes, she realised, green and guarded but infinitely beautiful. 'How could you be scared of something so precious?'

'Sotell.' Bailey looked frantically up to his uncle. *'Sotell,'* he said again as Lydia gave a bemused look.

'Show and tell,' Corey translated. 'They do it each week at kindergarten. One of his little buddies bought in a new sister last week.'

'Best get you to the hospital, love,' the paramedic broke in, 'and get this little lady checked over.'

'Come?' Lydia asked, blushing at her own presumption, then biting on her lip as Corey shook his head.

'I'll stay here and clear up and I'd best get Bailey home. Mum's coming over to look after him. I'm on nights tonight.'

Lydia nodded, tears dangerously close now, but not the happy tears of a moment before, just an aching gaping hole for all she had lost, all she had left behind.

'I'll come and see you,' Corey offered, 'before I start my shift, if I get there in time, or later on my break.'

Lydia nodded, though her heart was bleeding. She thanked him, said goodbye and wished she didn't have to. She didn't want him to come and visit her, didn't want him fitting her in around his shifts. She wanted him there with her, beside her in everything she did.

Finally realising what she had thrown away.

CHAPTER THIRTEEN

SHE was beautiful.

Seriously so.

For someone for whom babies were a large part of her life, Lydia had fretted over that initial greeting with her own child. Sure that the barriers she erected to deal with her fragile charges would remain intact, that she might somehow see her own infant as another rather sweet specimen. But her fears had been unfounded. Even after a very welcome cup of tea and the dimmed lights of her private room, courtesy of the fact she was one of the hospital's doctors, Lydia simply couldn't close her tired eyes. The sight of her daughter utterly captivating, lying safe and warm in the crib beside her bed, making little snuffling noises as she breathed, her tiny eyelids moving rapidly as she dreamed milky dreams.

Lydia stared, how she stared at the incredibly long fingers, nails that looked if she'd undergone some sort of miniature manicure to prepare her for her big date and dark curls that framed her petite pink face.

She loved her daughter, loved the emotion flooding through her, multiplying rapidly, and it was such a relief, so terrified had she been at her lack of maternal feelings, the silent doubts that had plagued her that it had been a mistake, the wrong time, should never have happened.

It had happened, and Lydia was so grateful for that,

grateful to finally close her eyes and let sleep wash over her, grateful for the joy of a daughter forever by her side.

Why she woke she wasn't quite sure. Exhausted, spent, nothing should have roused her, certainly not a tiny increase in her baby's breathing rate, the small snuffles louder now. Prodding around in her bed, she tried to find the call button, tried to remember where the light switch was located on the damn thing.

'Hey.' Smiling down at her daughter, she felt the first pings of over-reaction, chided herself at being a typical first-time mum, for there she lay, safe, asleep. Reaching out, Lydia gently clasped her daughter's slender fingers, her smile fading as she noted the slightly purple tinge, the dark nail beds, a notch of panic welling at the bottom of her throat, her heart rate picking up. She turned an anxious face to the young midwife who entered, turning on the main light and flooding the darkened room with bright fluorescence.

'How are you two doing?'

'I'm—I'm not sure,' Lydia stammered, berating herself but unable to hold back her concerns. 'She seems a bit...' Lydia's eyes took in her sleeping daughter, trying to asses her not as a mother but as a doctor. 'A bit cyanosed. Her hands are purple.'

'It's normal,' the midwife said, 'in the first few hours after birth. It takes a while for all the circulation to get going.'

'But she was pink before.' Lydia didn't look up, just carried on staring as the midwife came over, looked down at her infant, popped a tympanic thermometer in her ear. Lydia waited, waited for that wonderful patronising smile, the soothing words of comfort, to be told she was being over-anxious, it was all totally normal.

They never came.

'I'll just check her oxygen saturation.' The midwife pulled a pulse oximeter out of her tabard pocket, fixed the tiny probe to a tiny ear, and for the first time Lydia looked up, looked at the face of the midwife, desperate to see a relaxed smile on her face, appalled instead at the concern in her eyes, the rather more urgent movements as she unwrapped the baby, lifting up her tiny gown and watching the rise and fall of her chest.

'Her oxygen saturations are a bit low, Lydia. I might just move her over to the nursery and get the doctor to have a look at her.'

'He can look at her here.' Lydia shook her head, determined to assert herself, determined to keep her baby near her. 'I don't want her in the nursery. I want her beside me.'

But the midwife wasn't listening. There wasn't a trace of a reassuring smile. She just said something about 'popping' her on oxygen, not even moving the crib such was her haste to leave, just picking up the babe and leaving Lydia alone and confused with the vague order to 'wait here'.

Wait here?

What the hell was that supposed to mean? Shaking, Lydia poured herself a glass of water, barely able to get the glass to her lips her hands were trembling so much. She was over-reacting, Lydia insisted to herself, the midwife, too. She looked young, was probably just a student. She'd almost convinced herself, almost managed to calm herself down when she heard urgent footsteps, the rapid run of a doctor, a shrilling pager in his pocket, glimpsed not her own obstetrician but Dale Marshall, the night cover, flying down the hallway as he passed her door, stethoscope rattling round his neck. She waited, tried to reason he was on his way to a delivery, waited for this horror to pass, for someone, *anyone* to appear at her door, to smile and say it was all OK. But nobody came.

She wouldn't 'wait here'.

She was a doctor, for heaven's sake. They couldn't strap her to the bed, and she had every right to be with her daughter.

Her daughter!

The two words were enough incentive for assertion. On legs that felt like jelly she stood up, not caring that whether the ties on her gown were done up, not even giving it a thought. They *would* listen to her, they *would* tell her just what the hell was going on. But as the overhead intercom crackled into life, Lydia felt her knees buckle under her, willing it to stop, praying for it not to be true, while somewhere inside knowing it to be so. As the three chimes belled loudly she stifled a scream, rammed her knuckles so hard into her mouth she must surely draw blood, a whimper of horror strangling in her throat as the emergency call came.

'*NET's required, Nursery, Maternity Ward.*' The operator was speaking loudly, a touch breathless even. She was probably on her tea-break, perhaps having a chat as the call came through. '*Neonatal Emergency Team.*' Her voice was louder, more urgent as she summoned assistance. '*To the Nursery, Maternity Ward!*'

Lydia staggered out to the corridor, knees buckling under her, heading for the nursery, aware of running footsteps behind her. Staring through the glass of the nursery, she watched with horror the wheels moving into motion, the horrible ugly red crash trolley being pushed across the highly polished floor, the black of the cardiac monitor, the bright green signals of a heart rate going fast, way, way too fast, and somewhere in the middle of the chaos, somewhere in the middle of the tubes and machines, she glimpsed her baby. The skin that had been so pink, so warm, was purple now, mottled and grey, as if she'd been sitting too close to a gas fire. Legs that had been kicking, arms that had angrily pummelled the air around her were lying limp, like a washed-up frog, her head bobbing with each laboured breath. Lydia pressed her hands to the glass, watching Corey, *her* Corey, rushing in, working on *her* daughter, concern etched on his face, his mouth set in a grim line, then working its way into a shout, barking orders. Lydia had never witnessed Corey anything other than unflappable with a sick child.

'Stay calm, Corey,' she heard herself say, and even though there was glass between them she was sure it reached him, their eyes meeting for a fleeting anguished moment. 'She needs you to stay calm.'

He loves her, too.

It hit her then, right there and then in that lonely corridor, watching the man she loved battling to save a baby he loved, too, and she hated herself for pushing him away, hated herself for depriving her child and herself of the one thing they really needed.

'You can't be here.' The midwife was back, her voice kind but firm, taking her by the shoulders, leading her like a child waking from a nightmare back to bed. 'They're doing everything they can for her.'

'I need to be with her,' Lydia begged.

'I need to ask you some questions first,' the midwife insisted, 'then we'll see about letting you in.'

She wasn't a midwife, as it turned out. Lydia had been right with her first assessment. She was, in fact, a young student midwife called Nikki, who explained her qualifications carefully, whose hands shook slightly as she pulled up a chair and sat beside a shaking, pale Lydia. But she was kind and gentle and Lydia knew that her lightning reaction, her rapid assessment had maybe bought her daughter some time.

'Thank you,' Lydia whispered through pale lips. 'Thank you for coming in when you did, for getting help so quickly.'

Be nice, be nice. It was like a mantra going though her head. Maybe if she was nice, grateful, kind, they'd like her more, treat her daughter better. But nice didn't come into it. Lydia knew that deep down every baby was special, every infant precious, and all were treated as such.

'I'm sorry I can't answer all your questions,' Nikki said gently. 'The more experienced staff are with your daughter, but Dr Gibb asked me to check whether you were tested for strep B. We can't see a result in your notes, we're ringing the lab, but if you know the answer...'

'No.' Lydia's eyes were swimming with tears and she realised the ambiguity of her answer. 'I mean, no, I wasn't tested. My pager went off at my thirty-five-week appointment—we were going to do it the following week.' As the possible diagnosis sank in, the direness of her daughter's predicament was rammed home again with such appalling force Lydia truly thought she might vomit. 'Is that what they think she's got?'

'It's a possibility,' Nikki said. 'She's septic and having trouble breathing, and these sorts of infections generally transpire in the first few hours after birth…' A blush flooded her pale features and she apologised. 'I'm sorry. Of course, you'll know all this.'

'I don't know anything,' Lydia wailed. 'I don't know anything any more.'

Nikki's arms embraced her, but only for a fleeting second, holding her close for a tiny slice of time, but enough to help, enough to convey how much she cared.

'I have to let the doctors know what you've told me, but I'll be back as soon as I can.'

How long she sat there Lydia didn't know. Unblinking, she stared into the night, listened to the occasional sound of running feet, bit her nails down to the quick, retched in the semi-darkness as unthinkable thoughts invaded, wandering into the corridor then beating a hasty retreat back to her room, simply not knowing what to do.

'Dr Verhagh.' A smiling face was staring at her, a familiar face, and Lydia raked her mind, shaking her head in bewilderment as a the woman approached. 'I was just on the way to the nursery to give Paul a goodnight kiss, but apparently there's a sick baby in there. Poor little mite, they're running around like…' Her voice trailed off as Meredith finally registered the state Lydia was in. 'Doctor, whatever happened?'

'Oh, Meredith.' Lydia was sobbing as Meredith wrapped her arms around her. 'She's sick, so sick.'

'Your baby?' Meredith gulped. 'You had your baby? But she's not due yet. You only just left at lunchtime.'

Lydia gave a pitiful nod, 'I had her this afternoon. She was fine, she was beautiful, and now she's dying and I don't know what to do.'

'She isn't dying.' Meredith fixed her with a firm look. 'The doctors will be with her now, working on her and doing everything they can for her, just as you did for my baby.'

'She's dying,' Lydia intoned. 'I'm a doctor, I know how sick she is…' Hysteria was rising within her, her teeth chattering, knees literally buckling under her as Meredith grabbed her arms.

'She's going to be OK.' Meredith's voice was firm. She almost shook Lydia as she attempted to reach her. 'You're not a doctor tonight, you're her mother, and until someone comes and tells you that this is the end of the line, until someone senior comes and tells you that it's all over, you damn well be strong for her. You have to believe that she's going to get through this.'

Her words stilled Lydia and Meredith spoke more gently now.

'It's the only way you'll survive it, Lydia.'

Lydia nodded, looking at Meredith not as a patient's mother but as a woman who had ridden the emotional roller-coaster, one who was on the home run now but ready to share, to help a fellow passenger who had only just got on. 'I want to go to her.'

'Then go,' Meredith said simply.

Lydia shook her head. 'They told me to wait in my room, told me—'

'You more than anyone know what it's all about, and if you think you should be there, then that's what you should do.'

It seemed strange to be brushing her hair when her daughter lay dying, strange to be tying it back in a ponytail as Meredith rummaged in her bag and pulled out a smart navy robe. It was strange to even be thinking about putting on slippers at a time like this, but it was all with reason—they had to let her in, had to listen to her, and a deranged, hysterical post-partum mother didn't quite fit the dress code of a resuscitation scene. And with Meredith's help she got ready.

'Lydia.' Nikki's voice was kind as she walked into the nursery, but there was an edge of impatience to it. 'You should be in your room. Someone will be in as soon as they can.'

'I'm staying.' Not a tremble wavered her voice and even though she was intensely private, even though her darkest thoughts were hers, it was suddenly imperative they were shared, imperative everyone understood. 'I'm not going to get in the way, I'm not going to make a scene, but I really need to be here. You see, I'm not sure if she knows how much I love her.'

She could see Dr Browne shaking his head, could see her colleagues shifting uncomfortably, but just as the senior midwife opened her mouth to speak, to tell Nikki to take her back to her room, Jackie broke in.

'Lydia, she's very sick,' she said slowly. 'Very sick indeed.'

'I know that.' Lydia nodded. 'And I know that she

might die. That's why I should be with her, there for her. I haven't even given her a name.'

With infinite relief she watched as Dr Browne gave a brief nod, his attention immediately focusing back on the baby. Nikki's arms went around her, guiding her forward, not close enough to touch but close enough to be there. When Lydia glimpsed her daughter she'd have settled for the awful mottled purple of before, not the white, white porcelain doll that lay there, the fight gone out of her, a tube down her throat. Lydia could hear the hiss of the ventilator as it pushed air into her lungs.

'Push through a 50 mil bolus.' Dr Browne's orders were clear.

'She's bradycardic.' Corey's voice was urgent. 'Her heart rate's down to forty and dropping.'

'Emily.' Lydia's voice was a croak. 'Her name's Emily.'

'Come on, Emily.' It had been Lydia who'd said her name first but Corey who'd said it second, Corey whose fingers started cardiac massage on the slowing tiny heart as Lydia stood there, feeling as if her own heart was stopping too, watching the rhythmic massage, the controlled chaos of the nursery from a stool Nikki had gently lowered her into, praying and willing and making bargains she could surely never keep with a God that she couldn't believe existed.

How could he when her child was dying?

'Stop the massage.' Like everyone else she stared at the monitor, watching with relief as Emily's heart hit a stable rhythm. But there was no euphoria, just the hell of a never-ending roller-coaster ride, because Lydia knew if she knew anything at all that this was just the beginning.

Hopefully it was just the beginning.

'We're going to move her over to Special Care.' Corey was crouching down beside her, warming her pale hands with his, those beautiful green eyes that had loved her, adored her, been hurt by her, swimming with tears as he gently spoke. 'I know you need to be with her, Lydia, but you know we need an hour or so to set her up.'

'What if…?' She waited, waited for him to say it wasn't going to happen, but assurances were something that, however much they were needed, couldn't be given.

Not even by Corey.

'We'll get you.'

'No, you won't.' Lydia shook her head fiercely, but her voice was flat. 'She just about had a cardiac arrest, and you know as well as I do that if I hadn't been here no one would have come and fetched me.'

'Lydia.' Corey's voice was very firm but very gentle. 'You know how I run the unit; you know that I always get the parents, that it's my absolute priority. You will be there for Emily, whatever the outcome, but right now we need to get her settled and you need to make some calls.'

'Make some calls?' She stared. She could barely remember to breathe at the moment so the thought of holding a phone, dialling numbers, trying to somehow explain what she didn't understand herself, literally overwhelmed her.

'Ring your mum, she should be here with you.' He

cleared his throat, couldn't quite meet her eyes, and Lydia knew what was coming so she got there first.

'I've already rung him.' Lydia gave a tight shrug. 'And believe me, Corey, Gavin couldn't have been less interested. Emily doesn't need his apathy now. She needs positive vibes, people around her who love her…'

'He's her father.' There was a weary note of resignation in his voice, replaced in an instant by the efficient nurse that he was. 'I'll send someone to get you just as soon as we can.'

She hated making those calls. She could picture her mother standing in the hall, taking off her coat, jubilant from her brief visit to her new granddaughter. She hated hearing the joy in her mother's voice fade as an anguished whisper came down the line, the shock, the horror turning in an instant to a courageous strength, an unwavering bottomless river of love that mums somehow managed no matter the circumstances, promising to get there soon, promising to be there for her.

And then there was Gavin. Handing the number to Meredith, she dragged in some air as the numbers were dialled, explained as best she could just how desperately sick their baby was and then, when she'd said all she could, when sobs took over, she finally gave in and gestured for Meredith, who had been her pillar tonight, to take the phone.

'Is he coming?' Meredith's question wasn't nosy, just a natural reaction as she took the receiver from a bereft Lydia and replaced it.

Lydia shook her head, running a dry tongue over even drier lips, the shock still reverberating in her mind at Gavin's cruel dismissal. 'He says that he'll ring in the morning.'

She registered the shock that Meredith struggled to hide as she tucked the blanket around Lydia's shoulders. 'He knows how sick Emily is?'

'You heard me,' Lydia said flatly, staring at the dark window, watching the moon drifting behind a cloud, the darkness more fitting and perhaps more poignant with no glimpse of a silver lining. 'I don't think I could have made it any clearer. Anyway, Emily doesn't need him. She needs to feel love and peace and to be surrounded with positive thoughts.' Tears were splashing down her face as Meredith held her hand, not as a patient, not as a friend, just as a fellow mother.

'You're right,' Meredith comforted her. 'Emily doesn't need someone like that!' She gave a soft laugh. 'So much for my intuition. I thought Corey was the father.'

'Corey?' Lydia sniffed loudly. 'What on earth gave you that idea?'

'You two did.'

Lydia gave a weary sigh, meeting Meredith's eyes for a small slice of time. 'We're could-have-beens.' She saw confusion flicker in Meredith's eyes. 'Could have been, would have been,' Lydia explained softly, 'if it hadn't all been so complicated...'

'Should have been,' Meredith finished gently.

It was the longest night of her life.

Her mother arrived, with a flurry of tears and questions which Lydia simply couldn't answer. How could she explain what she didn't understand herself? That her gorgeous, beautiful, vital daughter, who had en-

tered the world healthy and crying, now battled for
her life only a corridor away. Some time later, Lydia
truly didn't know when, she was led along the still,
silent, night corridor and gently guided to wash her
hands. It was a routine as familiar as eating, so why
couldn't she work out how to pump the soap, why
couldn't she even reach for a paper towel?

And then she was beside Emily, physically anyway. Emotionally, since their first meeting, since
she'd held her, seen her, felt her, Emily had been
embedded in her heart. But the eyes that had know-
ingly gazed were closed now, shuttered with hospital
tape. In a way Lydia was relieved, relieved of being
spared the agony of that gaze, so bright, already so
familiar, undoubtedly blank now.

'Touch her,' Jo said gently, lifting one of Lydia's
hands and moving it beside Emily. 'Touch her and
talk to her. Let her know that you're here.'

Lydia wanted to touch her so much, wanted to feel
that soft, soft skin beneath her fingers, but her hands
bunched nearby, the familiar monitors alien now, loud
and terrifying, and a strangled sob parted Lydia's lips
as she pulled her hand away. 'I did this to her,' she
sobbed, rubbing her hands on her thighs, then wring-
ing them together as if she were contaminated. 'This
is all my fault.'

She saw the discomfort in Jo's eyes, even summoned the strength to feel sorry for her, knew how
hard it would be in her shoes, watching a colleague,
a strong, distant woman, dissolve before you.

'I did this to her,' Lydia repeated, but Jo shook
her head.

'Don't do this to yourself, Lydia.' Jo gave her shoulder a gentle squeeze. 'I'll get Corey for you.'

Only then did it register he wasn't around, only then did it strike her as strange that he wasn't looking after Emily. Sure, he was the NUM, but on night shifts he was a nurse, so why wasn't he here? Why wasn't the most senior, the most competent member of staff looking after her precious baby?

'Lydia?' She could hear the emotion in his voice, was vaguely aware of Jo moving to the other side of the incubator, giving them some space but ever close for Emily. 'This isn't your fault.'

'Then whose is it?' Exhausted, agonised eyes met his. 'Dr Hamilton offered me the test at thirty-five weeks, but my pager went off.' She shook her head. 'No, the truth is it had nothing to do with my pager going off—that was just an excuse. The truth is that because I hadn't shaved my legs, because I figured we could do it later, I turned him down.'

'You didn't know she was going to come early.'

'That's no excuse.' Her words were a brittle whisper. 'It's a simple swab, for heaven's sake, Corey, a two-minute test, and if I'd known I was a strep B carrier they'd have given me antibiotics and Emily wouldn't be...' She rammed her knuckles into her mouth and after a moment Corey pulled them away, holding her hand. Though she couldn't look at him, her eyes fixed on her daughter, she was aware of the weight of his gaze.

'Please, don't go there, Lydia. This isn't about blame, this isn't about fault. You know as well as I do that the tests aren't always conclusive, that even if you had been diagnosed as having strep B, there

was still only a small chance of Emily contracting it.'
His words may have been true but they bought no
comfort. 'Even if you had known,' Corey continued,
'it wouldn't have made any difference.' He watched
the tiny furrow of her brow. 'She came too quickly,'
Corey pointed out. 'There would barely have been a
chance to get IV access, let alone a dose of penicillin
in. You practically delivered her yourself.'

His words made sense, hit home just a little, but
still the frown remained, still the weight of guilt lay
heavily on her shoulders.

'They'd have been watching her more closely...'
Lydia started, but her voice trailed off as Corey
squeezed her hands tighter.

'Stop it, Lydia, stop it right now.'

'Why aren't you looking after her?' There was an
accusatory note in her voice, born of confusion, grief
and despair, a need to lash out, to apportion blame,
and if it couldn't be aimed at herself then the closest
adult would have to do. 'What were you doing holed
up in your office when you know you're the most
experienced nurse here, when you—?'

'I can't look after her.'

His words stilled her.

'The same way you can't, Lydia. I've called Joan
Watkins in to cover for me. I'm sorry, Lydia, I just
can't nurse her.' The frown was back between her
eyes and his hands reached out to smooth it, pulling
away at the final hurdle just as Lydia had done with
her child. 'I know she's not mine, I know that deep
down, but she isn't and ever will be just another patient.' Those strong shoulders were trembling now,
racked with grief and emotion, his voice a raw whis-

per. 'I'm sorry we can't be together, sorry that it can't work out for us, but it doesn't take away my feelings for you both and I just can't nurse her, I'm in too deep.'

'So am I,' Lydia wept. 'What I said before, back at the house, when I said that maybe we could—'

'Now's not the time.' Corey shook his head.

But now *was* the time, Lydia decided. She had to say what was in her heart. 'If Emily gets through this, if everything goes OK, maybe we can try again.' Her eyes darted with hope, but it was doused as Corey shook his head.

'Now's not the time to be making bargains with God,' Corey said sadly, and Lydia gave a mirthless laugh.

'Now seems exactly the time.' She screwed her eyes closed, realising how her words would have sounded—if Emily lived she'd take Bailey on, promise whatever it might take to get her baby through— but that truly hadn't been what she'd meant. The hope for a future with Corey that had imbued her only hours ago seemed ridiculous now. The excited plans that had started to form as she'd scrubbed the bathroom seemed as laughable as she must have looked.

Too little, too late.

She had lost him, and Lydia realised she had only herself to blame.

'You need to rest.' Corey broke into her thoughts, standing up as Joan came over. 'Joan's here now. I'll take you to the parents' room so you can lie down.'

'I'm not leaving her.'

'Yes, Lydia, you are.' Corey's voice was firm. 'You've just given birth, you're as white as a sheet.

You need to lie down and get some rest. If you stay here you're going to faint or something, and the staff need to be looking after Emily, not you. You'll only be a few steps away.'

She stroked the white petals of Emily's cheeks, tried to absorb every minute detail of that angelic face, murmured some words of love. Jo handed her some Polaroid photos. Glancing at them, Lydia wished she had some earlier ones and made a mental note to ask her mum to get the ones taken before the drama developed. She needed to be reminded, needed to witness again the beauty of innocence.

Like a child she let him lead her. Pushing open the parents' room door, she stared at the bland white furnishings, the hospital phone on a bedside locker. This was the room used for the parents of only the sickest of children. The others were housed in the old nurses' homes in the hospital grounds. As she lay down on the bed, closed her eyes in exhaustion, Lydia knew no strings had been pulled. She wasn't being put in here because of her status.

Emily was as sick as a baby could be.

CHAPTER FOURTEEN

'I GOT you this.' Corey held up the mechanical breast pump, but Lydia listlessly shook her head. 'Jo says you should try it, that you'll be more comfortable once you've used it.'

No, she wouldn't, they both knew it deep down. Her milk had come in and her swollen aching breasts yearned, as did Lydia, for her baby, to feed her own child, to perform the most natural task in the world.

Was it really too much to ask?

'Is there anything else I can get you?'

How austere he sounded, how formal and distant his voice seemed compared to the loving man she had briefly known. Jerking her head up for a flicker of time, Emily, though always at the forefront of her mind, receded slightly as Lydia allowed herself a glimmer of what she had lost—a man who had truly loved her. A man who stood before her, unfamiliar yet never awkward in a smart charcoal grey suit, a crisp white shirt set off by a dark tie knotted around his thick neck. The tousled curls she had once run her hand through were combed down now, damp from a shower, wafts of aftershave doing battle with the sterile scent of the hospital, but she was too dammed tired to ask what the occasion was.

True to his word, Corey had taken himself off the roster, yet he had popped in yesterday, hovered for an awkward moment before leaving. She knew from the nursing staff's updates that he rang regularly.

It just wasn't enough.

'I'm fine,' Lydia replied stiffly, pleating the sheet methodically, unable to look at him and not break down.

'If there's anything I can do, you know you only have to ask.'

'Sure.' A low laugh, utterly void of humour, escaped her lips, but Lydia quickly righted herself. The bitter note in her voice was swallowed with an apologetic shrug. 'I'm sorry, Corey, I shouldn't be taking this out on you. But it's been two days now. Surely she should be picking up, surely there should be some sort of improvement?'

'There has been,' Corey pointed out. 'Her temperature and blood pressure are more stable...'

'But she's still just lying there. She's still on a ventilator, and when they took the tape off to bathe her eyes this morning there was nothing there, Corey, nothing—just a blank look. What if she's brain-damaged?'

'You know it's too soon to be making those sorts of calls. You just have to be strong for her.'

'I'm trying to be,' Lydia sobbed. 'It's just so hard.'

'You're doing wonderfully,' Corey insisted. 'Lydia, you've just had a baby. Most women are lying in bed barely managing to scrape on some make-up for their visitors, yet you've barely left Emily's side. It's OK to cry in here, it's OK to let go. That's what a parents' room is for, a place to come to when it all gets too much.'

'It is too much.' Tears were coursing down her

cheeks now, sobs engulfing her body, and she wanted to let go so badly, to tell the truth, to unload the truth that had plagued her for nine long months now, because keeping it in was just too dammed hard.

'I didn't want her, Corey.' Her words were strangled, short agonised rasps as she unburdened her soul, and so vile was the truth Lydia couldn't bring herself to look at him, couldn't bear to see the scorn, the pity in his eyes as she told him her innermost thoughts.

'Lydia, don't do this to yourself, don't go there again. You've already told me you got pregnant to save your marriage, that babies were way down on your list—'

'You don't understand.' She was shouting now. 'I resented Emily, the same way I resented Bailey, because without them I was sure we'd have made it. I kept wishing my pregnancy would go away, kept wishing it had never happened. Even when I was in labour I didn't want it to be happening.

'I never wanted a baby.'

Her eyes raked his, waiting for the impact of her words to generate a flinch, for a flicker of scorn to darken those eyes. But instead green eyes held hers, gentle and calm and filled with understanding.

'I didn't want her,' Lydia said again, in case he hadn't heard, scarcely able to believe his bland reaction. 'What sort of a person does that make me? What sort of a woman feels resentment for the child she's carrying? I felt cheated, abandoned—'

'You were.'

His words stilled her, calmed her outburst, stilled the tears as he slowly walked over. Sitting gently on the bed, he took her two cold hands in his.

'So you didn't want a baby, there's no shame in that.' He felt her stiffen but carried on. 'You're not the first woman to feel that way. Hell, scrub that, you're not the only person to feel that way. I felt exactly the same with Bailey. I had a good job, the life I wanted and suddenly I was faced with father-hood. And as much as I love him as much as it breaks my heart to admit it, I didn't want to go there either.

'But you were prepared to give it a go, prepared to save your marriage, and if a baby was what it took then a baby was going to happen. You *were* cheated, not only by Gavin but by Marcia too, cheated by your husband and friend. And when push came to shove, you *were* abandoned. Is it any wonder you didn't want to be pregnant? Is it any wonder you didn't want to have a baby?'

His words made sense, a tiny flicker of light in the dark, dark tunnel she felt entombed in.

'You may not have wanted a baby,' Corey contin-ued gently, 'but you want Emily.'

Tears were starting again, so salty, so laced with pain they stung as they trickled down her red swollen cheeks, his eloquence, his insight almost more than she could bear and still breathe.

'You want Emily, because she's not just another baby. She's your daughter, and somewhere between the ambulance and the hospital she became a person, a person in her own right, a little girl who has a mother who loves her.'

'Oh, I do,' Lydia sobbed. 'I love her, love her,' she repeated, swallowing air in as her jaw chattered, al-most retching with the agony of it. 'And I'm so scared I've left it too late to tell her.

'Dr Browne wants to talk to me.' She gave a small jerky shrug. 'Wants to talk to me away from the ward. We both know what that means.'

He didn't answer, just gripped her hands tighter. Lydia didn't dare look, didn't dare read in his eyes that he possibly knew something she didn't.

'There is one thing you can do for me.'

'Name it,' he said softly, and even though she knew it wasn't right to ask, even though she'd ended it, right now pride didn't get a look-in.

'I'm not sure that I'm up to his directness. If you could do your NUM bit, stay with me and soften the blows a bit.'

'Of course.'

'He has to go to the children's ward for a team meeting then he's coming back to talk to me.'

'Oh, Lydia.' She heard the apology in his voice before he'd even finished the two words. 'I can't stay till then, I really can't.'

'I shouldn't have asked.' she forced a brave smile, even managed a dismissive flick of her wrist. 'You've obviously got an appointment.'

And even though what Corey did, where Corey went was entirely his business, even though Lydia had been the one to end it, she couldn't help but feel let down at his refusal to stay, to be there for her in what could be the most difficult conversation of her life.

'It's Bailey,' Corey started, but Lydia shook her head.

'You really don't have to explain.' She stood up crisply, wiped the back of her cheeks with her hands and headed for the door back to the unit, determined to escape with the tiniest shred of dignity.

'I'm due at the family court,' Corey broke in, over-riding her, taking her firmly by the shoulders. When she stilled, when he felt the tension seep a notch from her shoulders under his touch, he led her back to the bed. In the fog of her grief she'd forgotten just how important this day was for Corey and Bailey, and though her emotions were raw, her mind utterly saturated with her baby and her tentative hold on life, guilt touched her, guilt at the way she had dismissed their love for each other tinged with a flare of pride for the man who stood beside her now.

'I sign the papers for custody today. I just don't see how—'

'I understand.'

'If there was any way—'

'Corey, I understand.' Something in her voice reached him, something in her voice told him that perhaps for the first time she really did. 'You love him, don't you?' She watched as he simply nodded. 'No ifs or buts. You love Bailey. I can see that now. Maybe it took becoming a mother to understand it, but I finally do. You have to go to court, Corey. You can't let him down now.'

'Even if it means letting you down.'

A smile wobbled on her swollen lips.

'You've never let me down, Corey,' Lydia said softly, but as a tiny sob escaped his lips, as she watched that beautiful, strong face dissolve, she put a trembling hand to her lips, scarcely able to contemplate the depth of his pain.

'I have, Lydia, because I landed it all on you.

Implied you were the only one who was scared, that you were the only one with doubts, when the truth is I had them, too. I didn't know if I could do it, go from single guy to father of two. I was every bit as scared as you. And instead of telling you, instead of sharing, I let you take the blame, let you carry all the guilt for us breaking up. That night when you came, when you stood in the laundry and I told you how it was going to be, you didn't walk away, Lydia. I pushed you.'

'Why?' She stared at him, perplexed. 'Didn't you think I was up to it?'

'No!' The ferocity of his denial made her start and she sat there stunned as he turned agonised eyes to her. 'You deserved more, Lydia. You deserved a man that could love you, give you everything you needed, support you in everything. You deserved so much more.'

She blinked slowly, digesting his words before imparting her own. 'Everything you just listed,' Lydia said softly, 'you give to me, tenfold. You love me, support me, and right now that's everything I need.'

Her voice was clear, unwavering, and for the first time in days, weeks, months even, everything was finally clear.

'No one's to blame,' she said softly, her hands closing on his now, her eyes imploring him to listen, to understand, because finally she did. 'We were both scared, both cautious and we had every right to be. Gavin and I had no real problems, no real hurdles to face, and we still couldn't make it work. Most couples start off with a clean slate, with no choices to make other than the restaurants they'll eat in, yet for us two…' Her voice faltered for a second, the emotion catching up with her, and it was Corey who continued, Corey who carried on when it all got too hard.

'Maybe the hard times will bring us closer,' he ventured, testing the water slowly, watching as the hope that had died flared once again in her eyes. 'If we can survive all this, surely we can survive anything?'

She nodded, but words failed her, desperate to glimpse of a future with Corey beside her, Bailey, too, come to that, but terrified of a world that would be too big, too lonely without Emily beside her.

'We can make it.' There was a raw urgency in his voice but not a hint of a question. 'We can make it, Lydia, if we really want to.'

'I want to.'

It wasn't the most eloquent of answers, didn't come close to summing up her feelings, but the rest was there in her eyes, glittering with love and tears, joy and agony, with the weight of adulthood and the hope of a child.

'You'd better go.' It was the last thing she wanted him to do, the last thing she needed right now, and she saw the indecision in his eyes, knew the agony he felt on leaving her at this most awful time. It was her turn now to be brave.

'I'll ring the court,' Corey wavered, 'explain there's an emergency…'

'You can't do that to Bailey,' Lydia whispered. 'Today's his big day, his one shining light in two years of agony. And whatever today holds for Emily, for me…' She swallowed hard then somehow tendered a smile. 'For us—we'll face it. But right now you have to go to Bailey. That's what being a parent's about, Corey, putting someone else first, even if it hurts at the time. I'd do it for Emily and you have to do it for Bailey.'

'I'll be back.' Closing his eyes, he pulled her towards him, ran a rough cheek along hers, inhaling her scent as if it were the life force he depended upon. She breathed him in, too, dusted her salty, tear-soaked lips on his and held him for the tiny second the ticking click allowed.

'Go,' she gasped. 'But hurry back to me.'

Watching him leave was as bitter as it was sweet.

To have found him again only to lose him so soon was an agony in itself, yet it was tempered with hope, tempered with the promise of a love so true, so enduring that time seemed to take on no meaning.

Love is out there.

Recalling his words, this time they didn't scare her, this time they didn't mock her. Love was out there, not the love hearts and flowers and perfume kind, but a truer love that stood the tests, that even when it wasn't visible walked along beside you each and every step.

That made the world just that bit better.

Corey might have gone for a while but he would never, ever leave.

Pushing the parents' room door open, Lydia took a deep breath, ready now to face the world, to hold her daughter's hand whatever the outcome, to face the impossible while hoping for the improbable.

Corey's wide shoulders caught her eyes first, hovering over an incubator just as he had been the first day she had met him. Her heart quickened, anticipating the worst, sure only bad news could have halted him. But as she dashed over, as a strong arm pulled her in, Lydia knew there and then that all her prayers had been answered, that life had suddenly got better.

'I decided to call in a few favours.' His voice was thick with emotion as Lydia stood there stunned, staring incredulously down to where Emily lay. 'I figured Dr Browne was easier to negotiate with than a family court judge. I was hoping he'd move the children's ward meeting so that we could talk now.'

Still she didn't answer, still she gazed on to where Emily lay, pink and breathing, that delicious rosebud mouth free of tubes now, so divine, so delicious. Yet Lydia's gaze didn't linger. Instead it dragged up to Emily's eyes, knowing eyes that stared right back at her, eyes that held life and promise and a future there for the taking.

'I don't think there's any need to go behind closed doors now.' Dr Browne's voice was as formal as ever, as unwavering as ever, but his eyes when Lydia finally managed to drag hers away from her daughter's were kind. 'I have to say at this point that Emily was as sick as any baby I've seen, that this is an outcome I didn't dare to hope for...'

For a second he paused, just a tiny second when it wasn't a doctor talking but a fellow human being marvelling at the miracle of life, but he quickly righted himself.

'She's still a sick little girl, and all the questions you have up your sleeve, Lydia, you know I can't really answer. There is a chance there will be some developmental delays, deafness, some weakness. I don't need to reel off the possibilities, but from where I'm standing now...'

Still Corey's strong arms were around her as she inched forward, placed a trembling hand inside the incubator and marvelled at the soft, sweet skin beneath her fingers. Like a petal to the sun, Emily moved her cheek closer, nestled in the warmth of her mother's touch.

'From where I'm standing,' Dr Browne repeated, as Corey's grip tightened on hers, 'we can be cautiously optimistic.'

'I beg to differ, Doctor.'

It was Corey talking, but there was no insolence in his voice, just the jubilation of his smile.

'I think we can reach for the stars.'

EPILOGUE

'YOU'RE going to be late on your first day back at work.'

Blinking as the bedroom door flung open, Lydia winced as the landing light hit the rumpled bed. 'Five more minutes,' she groaned, pulling the sheet higher and trying to block out the light, but Corey promptly pulled it back.

'Some of us have been working all night,' he scolded, then relented. 'All right, five more minutes. I'll get you a coffee.'

Closing her eyes, Lydia attempted a return to her dreams, but a pudgy hand poking her cheeks soon put paid to that.

'Morning, Bailey.' Smiling, Lydia pulled back the sheet and finally gave in, sitting up just in time as Corey returned with a steaming mug.

'Room for one more?' Corey grinned. He climbed in fully dressed, then mouthed over Bailey's head, 'Was he wet?'

'No.' Lydia didn't lower her voice. 'Bailey was dry again, weren't you, Bailey? That's three nights in a row. He just didn't want to miss out on the fun when Emily woke for her five a.m. feed.'

They must have looked a sight. Corey in his uniform, Emily dozing on, Bailey jumping around the bed as Lydia sat semi-dazed with a boob falling out of her nightie as she sipped on her coffee. But not one of them would have had it any other way.

'How about I give Bailey his breakfast while you have your shower?' Corey suggested, noting the hesitancy as Lydia placed her empty mug on the bedside table. 'You're going to be fine.'

'I feel as if I've forgotten everything.'

'You'll be wonderful.'

'I don't want to leave her.'

'You'll be back at lunchtime,' Corey pointed out. 'And not a moment late, please. I've got another night shift to get through tonight!'

They'd attempted a roster, attempted to somehow put down on paper the impossible muddle of their lives as they juggled nursing shifts and kinder and breastfeeds, and from today a part-time doctor was being added to the list. But even a degree in logistics wouldn't have helped to plan this particular family's schedule.

'Come on, you.' Corey smiled. It's Bailey's special day.'

Bailey's very special day, Lydia thought some time later as she held his hand and clipped along the pavement in unfamiliar heels as Corey carried Emily. Today was show-and-tell day and for the first time in way too long Bailey had some good news to share with his class.

'Good morning, Lydia, you're looking very smart.' The smiling face of Mrs Mac greeted her as Lydia struggled to get an over-excited Bailey out of his jacket and shoes and into slippers.

'It's my first day back at work.' Lydia looked up and gave a small grimace. 'I'm terrified.'

'Rubbish,' Mrs Mac scolded kindly. 'You'll be

wonderful and you can tell us all about it when you pick Bailey up. Now, Bailey, Mrs Bartlett's waiting for you.' She smiled up at Corey. 'You too, so why don't you go and get ready for your big moment?' As Bailey scampered off to join the rest of his class on the mat, Mrs Mac called Lydia back. 'Now, did you remember that you're down for fruit duty on Thursday?'

She hadn't!

'The other mother can't make it so you'll be on your own.'

'But I've never done fruit duty,' Lydia moaned, terrified at the prospect of twenty-eight little people eyeing her efforts and, horror of horrors, sitting down to eat with them.

'There's nothing to it,' Mrs Mac rattled on, seeing Lydia's anxious expression. 'Bailey's looking forward to having you here for the morning and we can have a nice cuppa afterwards. Now, we'd better get this blessed show and tell over with so you can get off to work.'

It was miles away from where she'd imagined herself at this stage of her life, miles away from what she'd envisaged, yet Lydia loved every moment. Walking on tiptoe, Lydia slipped in quietly, glimpsing for a second the expectant faces gathered around the mat, but her eyes were drawn to one.

A little guy with gleaming hair, smart clothes and a proud smile so wide that if the power went off it would surely light up the whole of Melbourne.

'Bailey has something very important he'd like to share with us,' Mrs Bartlett, the kinder teacher, told the gathered children. 'Bailey, can you tell us who this is?'

Lydia smiled at Corey, unshaven and exhausted, his huge frame lowered into a miniature wooden chair holding up a rather restless Emily, but his smile was as wide as Bailey's.

'My baby,' Bailey said proudly.

'And what's your baby's name?' Mrs Bartlett prompted.

'Emily.'

'Is she your sister?'

There was always one, Lydia groaned, catching Mrs Mac's eyes frantically as a cheeky-looking red-headed boy stood up.

'She's…' Bailey faltered. 'She's Lydia's baby.'

'Is she your mum?' another child asked, and Lydia felt her heart plummet as twenty-eight pairs of accusing eyes turned to face her.

'Children.' Mrs Bartlett's voice was sharp, forcing the children's attention, dragging them back to face the front. 'Let's look at Emily's name bands from the hospital. When babies are born—'

'Is that your dad?' Clearly the little redhead hadn't finished and Lydia made a mental note to leave a pip in his orange next Thursday as Bailey blinked back threatening tears.

'Can I?' Corey's voice was low and quiet but Lydia stilled as she watched his lips move, watched as Mrs Bartlett gave a grateful nod as Corey pulled Bailey in beside him.

'You all know Bailey,' Corey said softly, 'and you've just met Emily. Perhaps we should introduce ourselves properly. I'm Corey, and over there is Lydia.' He gave a little wave and Lydia gave an awkward one back, her heart in her mouth, knowing this was too important to mess up, that today was so big, so vital for Bailey.

'Does anyone know what a family is?' Corey asked.

'A mum and dad,' someone shouted,

'Brothers and sisters,' a few more chorused.

'It can be.' Corey smiled. 'Some kids have a mum and dad, some kids have brothers and sisters.' He paused for a moment. 'Some don't.

'Everyone's family is a bit different. Families aren't just mums and dads and brothers and sisters, families are the people who love you no matter what you do, the people who you come home to at the end of the day and even if you're cross and a bit grumpy they still love you. Bailey has a mum who loves him very much, but she got very sick and couldn't look after him, but Lydia and I loved him so much we applied to the court to see if they'd let us look after him, and I'm very proud to say that they said yes.'

Oh, heavens, she was going to cry. Rummaging in her bag for a tissue, Lydia gulped thanks as a distinctly glassy-eyed Mrs Mac pulled a few out of the box, keeping a couple for herself.

'So,' Corey concluded, 'now we've worked that one out, maybe we can start again.' He gestured Lydia over. Blushing furiously, she joined him, smiling nervously at the expectant faces as Mrs Bartlett thankfully took over.

'Right, children, let's say hello to Emily, who Bailey's very kindly brought in for us to meet.' Taking Emily, she placed her on her knee, pulled back the bunny rug enough for the class to get a glimpse of her pretty pink face, her knowing eyes, blinking as she surveyed the world around her, a world she was starting to explore, doing everything a three-month-old should. Lydia thought her heart might burst with pride as Mrs Bartlett carried on talking.

'Emily's a part of a very special family.'

Your opinion is important to us!

Please take a few moments to share your thoughts with us about Mills & Boon® and Silhouette® books. Your comments will ensure that we continue to deliver books you love to read.

To thank you for your input, everyone who replies will be entered into a prize draw to win a year's supply of their favourite series books*.

1. There are several different series under the Mills & Boon and Silhouette brands. Please tick the box that most accurately represents your reading habit for each series.

Series	Currently Read (have read within last three months)	Used to Read (but do not read currently)	Do Not Read
Mills & Boon			
Modern Romance™	❏	❏	❏
Sensual Romance™	❏	❏	❏
Blaze™	❏	❏	❏
Tender Romance™	❏	❏	❏
Medical Romance™	❏	❏	❏
Historical Romance™	❏	❏	❏
Silhouette			
Special Edition™	❏	❏	❏
Superromance™	❏	❏	❏
Desire™	❏	❏	❏
Sensation™	❏	❏	❏
Intrigue™	❏	❏	❏

2. Where did you buy this book?

From a supermarket	❏	Through our Reader Service™	❏
From a bookshop	❏	If so please give us your Club Subscription no.	
On the Internet	❏		
Other _____		_____/_____	

3. Please indicate by number which were the 3 most important factors that made you buy this book. (1 = most important).

The picture on the cover	___	I enjoy this series	___
The author	___	The price	___
The title	___	I borrowed/was given this book	___
The description on the back cover	___	Part of a mini-series	___

Other _____

4. How many Mills & Boon and /or Silhouette books do you buy at one time?

I buy ___ books at one time ❏
I rarely buy a book (less than once a year) ❏

5. How often do you shop for any Mills & Boon and/or Silhouette books?

One or more times a month	❏	A few times per year	❏
Once every 2-3 months	❏	Never	❏

6. How long have you been reading Mills & Boon® and/or Silhouette®?
_____ years

7. What other types of book do you enjoy reading?

Family sagas eg. Maeve Binchy ❑
Classics eg. Jane Austen ❑
Historical sagas eg. Josephine Cox ❑
Crime/Thrillers eg. John Grisham ❑
Romance eg. Danielle Steel ❑
Science Fiction/Fantasy eg. JRR Tolkien ❑
Contemporary Women's fiction eg. Marian Keyes ❑

8. Do you agree with the following statements about Mills & Boon? Please tick the appropriate boxes.

	Strongly agree	Tend to agree	Neither agree nor disagree	Tend to disagree	Strongly disagree
Mills & Boon offers great value for money.	❑	❑	❑	❑	❑
With Mills & Boon I can always find the right type of story to suit my mood.	❑	❑	❑	❑	❑
I read Mills & Boon books because they offer me an entertaining escape from everyday life.	❑	❑	❑	❑	❑
Mills & Boon stories have improved or stayed the same standard over the time I have been reading them.	❑	❑	❑	❑	❑

9. Which age bracket do you belong to? Your answers will remain confidential.

❑ 16-24   ❑ 25-34   ❑ 35-49   ❑ 50-64   ❑ 65+

THANK YOU for taking the time to tell us what you think! If you would like to be entered into the **FREE prize draw** to win a year's supply of your favourite series books, please enter your name and address below.

Name: _____

Address: _____

_____

Post Code: _____ Tel: _____

Please send your completed questionnaire to the address below:

READER SURVEY, PO Box 676, Richmond, Surrey, TW9 1WU.

THE SURGEON'S FAMILY WISH by *Abigail Gordon*

Dr Aaron Lewis is captivated by new paediatric surgeon Dr Annabel Swain—especially since she's saved his daughter's life! He senses that Annabel, like him, has lost a loved one and is longing for a family. He's determined to help her overcome her past—but first he has to convince Annabel to share her secrets…

CITY DOCTOR, OUTBACK NURSE by *Emily Forbes*

Flight Nurse Lauren Harrison was stunned when flying doctor Jack Montgomery walked back into her life, six months after their brief affair. Attending medical emergencies together made it impossible for Jack and Lauren to deny their attraction—but for Lauren the question now is, how long would this city doctor last in the Outback?

EMERGENCY: NURSE IN NEED by *Laura Iding*

Past feelings are reawakened for critical care nurse Serena Mitchell when her ex-fiancé, Detective Grant Sullivan, is brought into the trauma room. She broke off their engagement when he refused to quit his dangerous job—and now her fears have been proved right. But caring for Grant is difficult for Serena – does she still have feelings for him?

Don't miss out…

On sale 1st October 2004

FREE!

4 Books
and a surprise gift!

We would like to take this opportunity to thank you for reading this Mills & Boon® book by offering you the chance to take FOUR more specially selected titles from the Medical Romance™ series absolutely FREE! We're also making this offer to introduce you to the benefits of the Reader Service™—

- ★ FREE home delivery
- ★ FREE gifts and competitions
- ★ FREE monthly Newsletter
- ★ Exclusive Reader Service offers
- ★ Books available before they're in the shops

Accepting these FREE books and gift places you under no obligation to buy, you may cancel at any time, even after receiving your free shipment. Simply complete your details below and return the entire page to the address below. You don't even need a stamp!

YES! Please send me 4 free Medical Romance books and a surprise gift. I understand that unless you hear from me, I will receive 6 superb new titles every month for just £2.69 each, postage and packing free. I am under no obligation to purchase any books and may cancel my subscription at any time. The free books and gift will be mine to keep in any case.

M4ZEF

Ms/Mrs/Miss/Mr ....Initials ....

BLOCK CAPITALS PLEASE

Surname ....

Address ....

....

....Postcode ....

Send this whole page to:
UK: FREEPOST CN81, Croydon, CR9 3WZ